Title and Subtitle

Title: Living Consort

Subtitle: Collection book for Shape Shifter and Threesome Romantic Stories

From the Author:
Thank you for purchasing this book.

Table of Contents

Mines, Theirs, Our Love

Description

Candace is not what most people call popular with men. She spends most of her time working as a senior designer at a notable fashion company, but everything changes when she bumps into Marlon, to whom there is instant attraction. Candace is later paired to work with the contracted architect but resists his advances due to job-related regulations.

Stood up by her friend, Paul, the owner of a bar assists Candace after she becomes too drunk to take care of herself. This escalates into an act Candace regrets, fleeing the scene the following morning.

With a new outlook, Candace gives in to Marlon's advances and is stunned to find out how closely he is connected to Paul. However, the three have good chemistry and are having a pleasant time when they are interrupted by intruders. As Marlon and Paul defend her, Candace is shocked to discover that the two men have an even deeper connection. Can she accept what they offer or would she run from the discovery?

Chapter 1

A smile spread across Candace's face right before her eyelids fluttered open. Then it all rushed to her, and she sprang from her bed in a rush. She grabbed her phone from the nightstand near her bed, then rushed to the bathroom of her single room apartment. She didn't need the phone to tell her the time, though. The risen sun was enough to inform her she was late.

"I am so dead," Candace mumbled, splattering toothpaste all over the sink.

Candace had been working with her company for five years, long enough for her to know that her boss did not condone tardiness. The first time she was late, she was still an assistant and the speech she received from her then supervisor was enough for her to ensure she was never late again. Until now.

Within a minute, Candace was out of the bathroom, her hair falling to her face in its drenched state.

It was times like those it thrilled her to be living in an apartment smaller than her childhood bedroom. Everything she needed for a speedy departure was well within reach.

Candace pulled on her trousers without ironing them. Luckily it was a stretched material, so the wrinkles didn't look too pronounced. Her blouse, however, was a different story, so Candace settled for a simple t-shirt tucked inside her trousers. It fashioned well with the white sneakers she wore.

Usually, she wore makeup, keeping it light, but today she opted out of it completely, settling for a small gold stud to accessorize her outfit.

Candace was already outside her apartment when she remembered the folders and samples she had brought home with her the day before. Scrabbling back into her apartment to retrieve them and released her first sigh of the day. The first of many.

The bus she took every morning to work had already passed, and the next one was fifteen minutes away. Candace couldn't wait that long, so she opted for a taxi instead, spending the money she had catered for her lunch for the ride to work.

It was the peak of the morning rush and traffic was backed up on all the streets. Drivers honked their horns loudly even though the act had no effect. Vehicles had nowhere to go.

"Just drop me off here," Candace said, as she stuffed a clump of cash into the driver's hand. The elderly man widened his eyes as she sprang from his car, folders in hand.

Candace zoomed across veterans' park to emerge on the intersecting street with sweat trickling down the side of her face. She was breathless, which only served as a reminder of how out of shape she was. Going to the gym was always delayed when she had extended workdays, and Candace almost always had an overflowing workload. After a while, she gave up on the gym completely.

Releasing a loud breath as her work building came into view, Candace pushed through the pain of her constricting lungs and heavy feet to shorten the distance to the building. A smile was on her face as she peered through the glass, noticing several of her coworkers entering the elevator. She should have kept her eyes on her path. If she did, she wouldn't have collided, falling to the ground with all her contents.

"Are you ok?" From where she sat on the concrete, Candace raised her gray eyes to meet the striking green ones of a tall but handsome man. He held out his hand to help her to her feet, but she couldn't get past his light blonde hair and pronounced jawline. The man had a smile drawn across his lips that was not seductive, yet a sensation tickled Candace's center. "Maybe I should call an ambulance."

Shaking her head out of her daze, Candace accepted the hand she was offered. "No, no, I'm fine," she announced, ignoring the ache in her ass. "I'm sorry I didn't see you there. Are you ok?"

The man chuckled, and it made his features even more attractive. "You're the one that fell, but you're worried about me?" He tilted his head. "What's your name?"

Candace opened her mouth, but her name got caught in her throat. Having this man so close to her was rattling her insides. "Candace. My name is Candace."

"Well, Candace, you sure do have a lot of tools," the stranger said, teasing in his voice.

Candace followed his eyes to where her belongings scattered around them; papers, fabric, and the tools needed to strip them.

"Oh," she gasped and dropped to her knees to retrieve the materials. "These are for work."

The stranger was also helping her to pick up her stuff. "I take it you work in the fashion industry."

Candace tilted her head, her mind blown. "How did you guess?"

The man stood tall now, his features even more handsome, with the sun highlighting them. "Well. For one, those papers have dress designs and we're standing in the middle of the fashion district."

"Oh," Candace said, her face becoming flushed. It was then she remembered the reason she bumped into this man in the first place. Candace edged toward her office building. "I'm sorry I have to go. Thank you for everything," she yelled behind her as the distance between them grew wider.

Just before the long hand on the clock in the lobby showed 9:00 am, Candace placed her ID card against the card reader. With a little luck and a whole lot of endurance, she made it just in time.

Tossing the documents onto the desk in her small office, Candace logged on to her computer, getting ready for the long hours ahead. She had not even finished prepping when the office phone rang. Candace answered the phone with an enthusiasm that deflated when she heard her boss' voice.

"Miss Bartholomew," the woman said in a sharp tone. "I need you in my office now."

The phone cut off before Candace even had a chance to respond. Instead of leaving immediately, she sank into her chair, using the moment to recuperate and frame her mind for the encounter.

"Candace, you're here," Sarah Andrews announced after Candace walked into her office. "Allow me to introduce Marlon Henson. Marlon is the architect designing our showroom."

The woman then addressed the man, staring at Candace with striking green eyes. "Marlon, this is Candace Bartholomew. She'll be your consultation for this project."

Candace was still enthralled by the stranger, a stranger she ran into on the streets not too long ago, when her boss' words finally sank in. "You want me to what?" She forced her eyes away from the third occupant, his presence overpowering even with her boss' commanding eyes piercing her.

"I want you to be his consultation for this project. We have a certain requirement as designers and I'm putting you in charge of keeping him in the know." Sarah's voice was firm, which hinted at a finality.

Still, Candace had to at least try. She was swamped enough at it was. Adding another task to her day would deprive her of even more sleep. "Ms. Andrew. I am already strained. Maybe one of the junior assistants can take this task. I know they would be happy for the opportunity."

"There is no way I can give this responsibility to a junior designer." Sarah's eyes were intense. "This room would be with us for a long time and I don't think they can help capture the idea of our brand. Not the way you can."

Sarah had a point. The company would be stuck with the showroom even if the designers did a poor job. It was best to let someone much more capable handle it. Although she didn't understand why it should be her. Sarah was in a much better position to deal with the design. She was the boss, after all. "I understand that, but it's just that I already have so much work on my schedule. I can't possibly fit something else."

Sarah looked at Candace with narrowed eyes, annoyed that she was doing this in front of the company, but if Sarah had considered informing her beforehand, they would have had the conversation then.

"I don't care what you do. You can give one of the others a lesser important project for all I care, but you *are* handling this." There was irritation in her voice as she spoke now, and Candace knew better than to aggravate her any further.

"Yes, ma'am," she complied with her hands in her lap and her head slightly low. "I'll see to it."

"Great." The single word was one of dismissal, and Candace nodded to her new partner before leaving the office.

As she walked out, Candace heard her boss giving Marlon his last instructions and Candace's contact information. She pushed out her lips as creases formed on her forehead. With this added project, Candace was not going to get any sleep.

Chapter 2

"Ok, so here is closest to the window and should be able to fit at least five mannequins. We want to be able to fit five outfits from the same line." Candace flicked through the papers on her desk, seemingly searching for something. "This display is the most important since it gets clients inside the building." She released a heavy sigh and slammed the folder closed. "I must have left the samples in my office. If you can give me a minute." She pushed herself from the leather chair in the conference room. "It will only take a minute."

"But unnecessary." Marlon held her in place, the spot where he clung to her wrist tingling from his touch. "I understand completely. Please." He released her hand and pointed to the chair. "Let's continue."

Candace was hesitant, more because of the strange sensation overwhelming her now than the possibility of her needs being misunderstood. Still, she sat, her eyes taking in everything other than Marlon's.

"So I was thinking about rising this area at the entrance." One eyebrow was raised as Marlon highlighted the area in the diagram on the tablet. "Maybe I'll layer it like steps so mannequins can be displayed on each layer."

Candace's eyes were wide now. She couldn't believe how in-tune with displays this architect was. With him spearheading the display room, her presence was unnecessary. "And it would also highlight the outfits displayed there. That's a great idea."

Marlon smiled, and it tugged at Candace's heart. *Why is he so sexy?* At that moment, all she wanted was to be closer to him, to feel the warmth of his body engulfing her. With her throat suddenly dry, Candace pushed away from the striking man at her side, pushing strands of loose, straight blonde hair behind her ears. It was an act that found Marlon's attention and the amusement in his eyes was unwaveringly apparent.

When it came to men, Candace was vastly inexperienced. She was drawn to Marlon in a way that was unfamiliar, yet she did not know how to act. The knowledge of her attraction made her even more awkward and her clumsiness peered through. With no genuine experience with men, at the age of thirty, she felt like an outcast, doomed to spend her days at her desk completing endless tasks.

Burying her emotions behind her work, Candace continued with her consultation. "For every line, we usually come out with beachwear, so I was thinking of dedicating an entire section to this."

Marlon stared at the preliminary designs. "I think building this area," he pointed to the tablet. "Surrounding it with glass so that the sand wouldn't get on everything."

"Sand?" Candace tilted her head.

"It's beachwear right?" Marlon's lips were slightly curved. "What's a beach without sand? I think it would add an extra touch to the display room. Don't you think?"

Candace couldn't believe she never thought of this. "Yes, it would. That's actually a marvelous idea."

Her statement prompted a chuckle from Marlon. "Well, I like to surprise others with my ingenious ideas now and again." After a few seconds, he asked, "What are you doing later?"

Candace jolted upward, his question seemingly coming from nowhere. "I'll probably be working. I'm really busy these days." Her words were unsure.

"You can't work all the time. You need to have a little fun now and then." Then Marlon's lips twisted, his eyes piercing hers. "A friend of mine owns a bar. Why don't we go?"

"You mean—together?" Candace's eyelashes fluttered rapidly.

A chuckle escaped Marlon. "Why not? I'm good at other things besides work."

For a moment, Candace wanted to give in to his request. She wanted to be spontaneous for once and forget all her responsibilities. But she couldn't. Actions had consequences, and she didn't want one moment of weakness to affect her for the rest of her life.

"I can't," she said, her heart aching as the words came out of her mouth. "We should keep our relationship strictly professional."

Marlon looked at her, his eyes etching her skin. "Is there anything wrong with us becoming friends?"

"If my boss finds out, I'll be in trouble." Candace wasn't lying. Fraternization with clients was strictly prohibited and if she was caught, it could cost her a job. Still, that was not the main reason Candace rejected Marlon's offer. This man had a presence that overwhelmed her, causing reactions to her body, and that scared her.

Marlon tilted his head, a slight smile on his lip. "Well, just don't let her find out."

It was a tempting offer, but Candace had to decline, her mouth twitching as she did so.

Candace was still going over the conversation with Marlon in her head later in the afternoon when her phone rang. "Hello?" she answered without watching the number.

"Candace," her friend Laura spoke in a high-pitched voice with a dragging drawl. This could only mean one thing. She wanted something.

"Whatever it is Laura, the answer is no," Candace said the firm, her fingers flicking through pages as she pressed the phone to her ears with her shoulder.

"But you don't even know what I want yet," her friend whined.

"It doesn't matter," Candace said. "If you need to sway me, then you know it's something I don't want to do, so forget it."

The other woman continued to whine. "But I'm meeting a guy I met on TikTok for the first time tonight and I need a buffer."

Unlike Candace, her friend Laura was extremely outgoing, dating almost every week, usually with different men. Their friendship was unusual - as the women were so different - but they had a common interest. Both women were different from their peers, so they found solace in each other.

"I don't want to end up with a stalker or something," Laura argued.

"Well, here's a tip." Candace held the phone with her hand now. "How about you don't date people you meet on social media?"

"But the men I usually meet in person are so *boring*." The woman's words were so high-pitched that Candace had to pull the phone away from her ears. "I just need my best friend to have my back." Then she said in an almost babyish tone, "What do you say, bestie?"

Candace took in a sharp breath and released it with a force. "Fine. But this is the last time." That were the same words she used the last time Laura forced her into an uncomfortable situation with one of her dates.

"Great. We'll meet at a bar that just opened up at eight. I'll text you the address." And without giving Candace time to change her mind, her friend ended the call.

Candace looked up at the clock on the wall. It was already 6 pm. She'll finish her work and head to the bar right after.

Chapter 3

The bar wasn't like any of the other bars Laura usually dragged Candace to. This one had a dark aura about it, something unnerving but also exciting.

As she walked through the door, she was greeted by a man who scanned her with a suspicious device. It wasn't a metal detector, but he used it in the same way before giving her a blue band. Candace dismissed her concerns. Maybe it was just a new version of the safety tool.

Inside was sectioned into three, the table area for those choosing to eat with their drinks, the bar counter if they are patrons who just wanted to drink, and a VIP section, where apparently only those with red bands were allowed.

Candace navigated through the packed bar, occupying the only available stool at the counter. From there, she scanned the room for her friend, who was apparently late. The sound of glass hitting wood directed her attention behind where the bartender was giving her his full attention.

He was a tall, muscular man with unique green eyes, eyes she only saw once in her life. The man had broad shoulders and a pronounced jawline with large hands. He was definitely one of the most handsome men she ever saw, but rugged.

"I didn't order that," Candace said, referring to the drink the bartender placed in front of her.

"I know," the man said, his lips curling to the side. "This one is on the house." Then he leaned in. "Only for a gorgeous lady like you."

Candace's jaw fell. She had never been complimented for her appearance before and especially not from a man that looked like him. Candace looked up at the man, wanting to trail her fingers in his rugged beard.

"I really shouldn't." She pushed the drink back to him, but he was not about to give in that easily.

"Of course, you can," the man said and offered the drink once again. This time he flashed her a smile, which had Candace thankful she was seated. Otherwise, she would have lost her footing.

She took the glass slowly and said, "Well, thank you for your generosity," before sipping the aqua drink.

The bartender kept his eyes on her. "I'm Paul, by the way."

"I'm Candace."

The man winked at her before leaving to attend to another customer, while Candace quietly finished her drink. By the time her drink had finished, there was another one waiting for her.

"Oh, no - no. I can't accept this." Candace shook her head but couldn't stop the smile from curling her lips. "This is too much." Then she pushed out her lips. "Your boss would be upset if he finds out."

Paul leaned in and whispered, "Then we just won't tell him."

It was strange hearing this phrase again. Candace wrapped her fingers around the glass as she remembered her conversation with Marlon not too long ago.

Noticing her blank stare, Paul continued, "If you don't take it, then I'll have to throw it out and he'll get even more upset. So do us both a favor and just accept the drink, ok?"

"Fine," Candace snapped out of her daze. "But no more ok."

"I can't make any promises," Paul said, walking away before she could speak again.

Maybe Candace should have found out the contents of the drink before consuming two glasses. She had never been able to hold her alcohol, and this time was no different. By the time her friend called her, Candace was already experiencing the effects of her mystery drink.

"So, I've decided not to go on the date after all," Laura began. "Meeting men on the internet is too dangerous and there are so many creeps out there."

"That's what I've been telling you," Candace said with a slur before pushing herself off the stool and heading to the bathroom. Her head spun slightly, and she wobbled slightly, drifting into a busty redhead. Candace apologized with a raised hand before continuing her phone conversation. "But you're still coming to the bar right. I'm already here."

"Uh, I don't think so. This man I met with last week called and he wants to go to a concert. I'm leaving my apartment now."

Candace was in line now, waiting for the person inside the washroom to vacate. "Are you kidding me?" she screamed at her friend over the funky rock song.

"I'm sorry love I'll make it up to you. Get home safe," Laura said before ending the call. Candace fumed as she entered the bathroom after the skinny man left.

She ran into the open stall, her phone still in hand as she bent over the bowl to release the unsettling contents of her stomach. There was no force involved, but Candace clung to the sides of the bowl until her phone slipped from her hand and into the water.

Candace just stood there for a while, with her eyes bulging, watching the device as it sunk to the bottom. In her drunken haze, it was hard to decipher if her phone had actually fallen in, but there was no doubt about her dilemma.

Her first thought was just to abandon it. She could simply get a new phone with the same number the following day. But then she'll have to go through the trouble of reinstalling her contacts and she was expecting a call from

Marlon the next morning. What if he called and her phone was not operational as yet? If Sarah found out, then she would be in trouble. And she would just feel empty without her phone.

No. She had to get it back, but that was something easier said than done. Candace couldn't bring her hand to the bowl, no matter how hard she tried. Looking away didn't help. Her lids involuntarily opened.

Feeling beaten and overall exhausted, Candace allowed her body to settle onto the tiled floor with her back to the door, and slowly the world around her disappeared.

Chapter 4

"Hey, Paul," Jake, a friend of the man, said, "we've got a problem in the bathroom. A lady passed out in the stall."

"Dammit," Paul muttered under his breath as he dropped the glass in his hand and headed toward the unisex bathroom. As a bartender for many years, he had seen a lot of things and now that he owned his own bar, he didn't expect things to be any different. Although he was taken aback by the woman on the floor. Straight blonde hair obscured her face, but there was no doubt. It was the woman he gave the drinks to before. But how was she passed out? She only had two drinks.

"Hey. The line outside is backing up. What are you going to do with her?" Jake was standing behind him.

"The same thing we do with all our drunk patrons. Call the last number on her phone." Paul angled himself to get a closer look at the woman, looking a bit erotic even in her sleep.

"That might be a little troublesome, man." Jake pointed to the phone soaking in the bowl. "I'm definitely not getting that."

The bulky man swore under his breath again, considering his option. He definitely couldn't leave her there. He couldn't bring her back to the main bar, either. The VIP room had long couches. She would be comfortable there, but judging by the band on her hand, which was not an option. There was only one place he could bring her.

Paul bent over and lifted the woman into his arms, momentarily taken in by her dazzling eyes. He then brushed past the people waiting in the line outside the washroom and at the back to his private quarters.

The woman didn't even stir, not even when he placed her on the bed and encased her in the covers. Paul took a minute to admire her before returning to deal with the situation she caused in the bathroom. Only after he was able to rejoin his employee behind the bar. Still, his thoughts remained on the woman at the back with her hair scattered about his pillow.

Images of her sultry skin smooth under his touch and her lips, subtle and kissable, teased him. Paul forced his eyes closed and then opened them again while shaking his head. Still, the naughty thoughts swirling around did not disappear. They remained the entire night, even as the bar became emptied as the night winded down.

Paul hesitated for a few seconds before entering the back room he called home. It was a small — a studio apartment—but it was his. He tried his best to turn it into a home, even splurging on the couch set, though he hardly ever used it. Paul was always on the move, organizing for his bar when he wasn't working in it. The little time he spent in his home was spent sleeping or entertaining a female companion.

He took in his guests' appearance once again. She was different from the women he was used to. More conservative, but he found that aspect about her aroused him. Even with her plain white blouse buttoned to the nape of her neck, she caused his manhood to twitch in his pants and his eyes to flicker.

Paul exhaled sharply, turning away from her to get a bottle of water from the refrigerator. He needed to calm himself, but the longer she remained in his presence, the more rattled he became. He needed to get her out of there.

He walked over to her, a determination on his face, shaking her vigorously. "Candace, wake up." The first few times he called, she didn't stir, but finally, she opened her eyes, capturing his green ones. When Paul felt the rise in his crotch, he knew he had to get her out of there before it was too late. This woman didn't travel with his type of crowd. She was innocent, and he wanted to keep it that way.

"Candace. It's late. Is there anyone I could call for you?" His words had an urgency, but Candace's eyes were wild, as if unable to decipher what he was saying. She couldn't possibly still be drunk. Not after two drinks.

"Candace," he said, nudging her shoulder, but his touch only made her eyes wilder.

Oh shit, he thought to himself. *If she keeps looking at me with those big, bulging eyes, I wouldn't be able to contain myself any longer.*

Candace did not know what she was becoming entangled in, yet she reached up to stroke behind Paul's neck and pulled him down for a kiss. She wasn't drunk. The alcohol had long worn out of her system. She was just tired. Tired of always holding herself back, not being able to do what she wanted.

Tired of being too cowardly to take the plunge. Sure, Laura was always getting disappointed by men, but at least she put herself out there. She was not afraid to strive for what she wanted, and Candace admired that. She wanted to be more like Laura and right now she wanted this delicious man with abs of steel.

Paul didn't need further nudging. His body sprawled over her as he clung to her waist, his touch rough but welcoming. Candace shivered under his touch, under the full length of his body and the feel of his hardened dick through his pants.

For a moment, he released her mouth, trailing kisses along her neck, and Candace moaned as he nipped her flesh. No doubt, Paul would make it an unforgettable experience. When his mouth returned to hers, his hands were underneath the hem of her skirt, reaching for her gentle folds. The sensation as his fingers slipped underneath her underwear to rub against her sensitive nub was overwhelming, causing her to wiggle underneath his touch.

"You're so wet," he said, his breathing heavy as he pierced her with intensity. "Come for me." His words were more of a command, which Candace obliged to once the movement of his fingers quickened. She held onto the bed, clutching it tightly as her body convulsed around his fingers, leaving her breathless.

Candace's legs were numb, but Paul was not finished with her. In fact, he was just getting started.

When he tugged at his shirt, buttons scattered about the floor, and the act seemed to create urgency in him. His pants were next and Candace gasped as his manhood sprung free, void of any underwear.

"It's not too late to change your mind," he said, comfortable in his nakedness. Candace couldn't speak. The most she could do was shake her head and the sexy man rid her of her clothing.

He didn't resume his position then. Instead, he flipped Candace over so her stomach rested on the bed, holstering her ass high. A sharp hand came down on her, causing her to cry out, but her cries were not completely out of pain. Candace realized she loved the feeling of being spanked and she loved it, even more, when Paul gripped her by the waist and entered her from the back.

With one fluid movement, he was inside her, cock twitching from her tightness. When he frowned, he aroused her even more, and Candace relaxed, allowing his manhood to better fill her up.

Like his entry, Paul's thrust was far from delicate. It was rough and sharp, pleasurable torture that caused her to scream with every movement. With his hand in her hair, Candace closed her eyes and pushed back on him, matching his intensity. Matching him stroke for stroke as he brought her to new heights.

Candace didn't believe it was possible for her to orgasm twice. None of her previous lovers had accomplished the task.

Yet, there she was, convulsing around Paul for the second time for the night. It was absolutely intoxicating, and Candace bucked, clutching the sheet until her knuckles turned white.

When Paul finally exploded in her, there was a force behind it and his fingers dug into her flesh. With a powerful grown, he emptied himself inside her, pushing even deeper until she felt him at her stomach.

Candace had never had sex like this before, and she wanted more.

Chapter 5

Candace's eyes fluttered open as memories of the night played through her mind. It was her intention to be impulsive, but maybe she was too impulsive. Had she really slept with a complete   stranger?

She peeked at herself, naked underneath the coverings. Then she tilted her head upwards to stare at the man whose chest was bare and legs dangled from underneath the sheet. She had definitely had sex with the sexy bartender. Candace flinched and clamped down on her lips.

What was she going to do?

There was only one thing she could think of. Make a speedy escape before he woke up.

Easing herself out of bed, Candace left her companion with the covers, too afraid to take them away from him. She skipped across the room, retrieving pieces of clothing from where they discarded them the night before, putting each piece on one at a time.

After Candace finished dressing, she looked back at the naked man. He was still asleep, giving her time to ease out of the small accommodation, softly closing the door behind her. When she was out of Paul's apartment, she breathed a sigh of relief and placed her hand on her chest.

Candace picked up the pace now, strutting her legs as she navigated between the tables and chairs stacked on top of them. She was in such a hurry that she didn't notice the huge bulk in front of her, bumping it to him with a force that sent her backward.

That appeared to become a trend.

Candace clutched her forehead - the area smacked by the man even bulkier than Paul - and rubbed hard.

"Watch it," the man said in a rough, rumbling voice, but there was a menacing look in his eyes. It made Candace shiver, but not in the same way Paul did. With this man, Candace wanted to cuddle up and hide.

"Sorry," she said, keeping her head low as she bypassed him and practically ran out of the building.

Outside, she was able to slow her breath and regain her composure. Candace took a few deep breaths and spoke to herself. "You're ok. It's fine. You never have to set foot in that place again."

Her ramblings were meant to reassure her, but they weren't very effective. Candace was still taken aback by the entire situation and shocked at herself.

As soon as her legs were steady enough to walk, Candace went to her apartment. It was not much different from Paul's as it was also a studio. However, hers was exquisitely furnished and had a feminine touch.

When Candace walked into her home, she walked into the sitting room. Here she had placed three couch sets, angled in a semicircle. They hovered around the space saver, which housed the television and the stereo. Candace kept a table with a small fish tank in the corner. She wanted a bigger one with more fish, but Beta fishes are known to be aggressive with other fishes. So she kept Sarah all by herself.

There was a protrusion to the left side of the house where her tiny kitchen stored everything she needed. Everything meant coffee. Since Candace was always working, she seldom spent time at her apartment and therefore rarely cooked. The kitchen shared space with the dining room, which meant Candace only had room for a two-seat set. This wasn't a problem for her since she rarely had a guest over.

Leading from the kitchen was a short walkway that extended into the bed area. With her full-sized bed in the middle, the area was almost filled. This was a sacrifice Candace was willing to make. She needed to have comfortable sleep, but what she didn't need was a lot of closet space.

Much to her friend's dismay, Candace kept her wardrobe simple, focused on plain and neutral-colored clothing with simple designs. Laura had tried multiple times to extend Candace's range, but she was unsuccessful each time. Candace simply tucked away all the clothing her friend bought her into the back of the dresser drawer.

The first thing Candace did after entering the apartment was to take a bath. She felt dirty and uneasy about her night activities and, therefore, drenched herself underneath the shower, letting the water run all over her body, soothing her nerves. Then she wrapped her blonde hair into a neat ponytail and clothed herself in blue jeans and a simple tank top with a gray hoodie. Candace grabbed an apple out of the fridge.

It was a Saturday, and she didn't have to work but had organized a meet-up with Marlon so he could show her his plans. On the way to the office she bought a hot cup of coffee, black, then strolled into the office with bags under her eyes and a scrunched-up face.

"Long night?" Marlon asked, his hands immediately pulling out the chair for her to sit.

"Extremely," Candace said, taking a sip of her drink while sitting on the chair. "I feel like I've been run over by a truck."

"Well, I'll make this short so you can go home and get some rest." Marlon spread his plans on the table in the conference room. "Ok, so this is what I have so far. If you agree with everything here, then I will go into more details."

Candace pushed forward in her chair, analyzing the drawings of the details they had gone through before. The entire time, Marlon sat watching her, with his lips curved into a gentle smile.

Suddenly, she felt self-conscious. "What is it?"

He shook his head. "Nothing. I just like watching beautiful things."

Candace's eyes widened at his words. Did that mean she was beautiful? She had never been told she was beautiful by a man before. Not even those she had slept with.

"Stop joking," she chuckled and tapped his arms. "I'm plain."

Marlon looked deeply into her eyes. "Sometimes plain is better. Like vanilla ice cream." He reached out and touched her arm. "And I love vanilla ice cream."

When Marlon touched her, Candace's heart started to escalate, but not the same way it did when she was with Paul. With Paul, it was mostly lust, a feral attraction to a very sexy man, but with Marlon, it was much more, an inner connection, entangling their souls. Both men were completely different, and she felt differently about them. With Paul, she wanted to screw hard, but with Marlon; she wanted to make love and cuddle.

Still, what kept her from accepting Marlon's offer was still an issue. He was related to work and, therefore, untouchable.

Candace pulled her hand from his reach, and the moment she did, she felt an emptiness. "You incorporated my suggestions beautifully. I have no alterations to this design."

What else did she expect? With Marlon, it felt like they were in sync, knowing exactly what the other wanted. If that was true, then he must feel what she felt every time they were close to each other.

"How about dinner?" Marlon leaned in, his eyes wide.

"You know I can't do that," she responded, putting her bag on her shoulder.

"What's wrong with grabbing a bite after work?" Marlon's head was tilted. "Aren't co-workers allowed to eat together?"

Candace eyed Marlon for a long time. Despite everything, she wanted to spend more time with him. Last night, she broke the rules and had sex with a sexy stranger. Why not bend the rules some more?

"Just dinner?" she asked, her eyes wide as her head jerked backward.

"Just dinner," he said, his hands against his chest. In his mind, he was saying, today dinner, tomorrow something else.

Chapter 6

"Do you have any place in mind?" Marlon asked, but Candace kept her lips sealed and shook her head.

She couldn't tell him the last time she went out to a restaurant was before her boyfriend brutally dumped her for another woman. That was two years ago and since then she hadn't been with anyone, except for the sexy bartender.

"That's alright." Then he snapped his fingers. "I think I know the perfect place. Do you like Mediterranean food?"

Candace's face lit up, and she felt energized. "It's actually my favorite."

"Then you would love this place." Marlon grabbed her hand, and his touch made her flinch. She loved it. "Come on."

Marlon took Candace to a cozy restaurant, fifteen minutes onto an isolated road. And like a gentleman, he opened the door for her to get out of the car.

"Look at that," Candace said, her head upward into the night sky. "There are so many stars. It's beautiful."

"The scenery is one of the things I like most about this restaurant," Marlon said, leading her to the balcony. "When you taste the food, you will understand the second."

It was a magnificent restaurant with low lighting and a simple yet intricate setting. The theme was natural and earthy, with the fresh mountain air enriching the patrons.

Marlon guided Candace to a seat on the balcony, holding the chair out for her. "How did you find this place?"

He sat down opposite her as she scanned the surrounding trees and the fireflies that darted through them. "A friend of mine owns it."

"Not all of it." Candace and Marlon both turned their heads to the dark-haired man as he approached. "Marlon," he said to his friend. "I haven't seen you in a while. Came to check on your investment?"

Marlon greeted his friend and then introduced Candace. "Henry is the owner of the restaurant and the best chef there is."

"Come on, man. You don't have to say that." Then Henry turned to Candace with a grin on his face. She couldn't quite decipher it, but there was meaning there. "But he's right. I am."

"Oh, so modest." Marlon's sarcasm was obvious. "Just treat us good tonight, OK?"

"Don't I always?" Henry raised his eyebrows. Before he left the table. "Don't worry, I'll make it a meal you can't forget."

It was hard not to smile in such a magnificent place. "You guys seem close," she said, referring to Henry and Marlon.

"Yes, we are," he responded. 'It's a bunch of us, actually. We grew up together and remained friends."

Candace couldn't imagine having that many friends. "That must be nice. I didn't have many friends going up. Nobody wanted to hang out with the weird one."

"Well, it's their loss." Marlon held her gaze. "Because you are an absolutely wonderful person."

Candace smiled, her eyes sparkling under the crescent moonlight. "You barely know me."

"I know enough to realize that you are a caring, intelligent, and heartwarming person. There is a quiet nature about you, but I can sense that you're far from quiet when your loved ones are involved." Candace tilted her head, her forehead scrunched and mouth slightly open as Marlon continued. "I've been interested in you since the first time I saw you. Of course, I've been paying attention."

Her words caught in her throat, and it took a while to get them out. When she did, every word sounded like a surprise. "You're interested in me?"

"Wasn't it obvious?" Marlon straightened himself. "Well, let me make it clear so that there is no confusion." He took her hand, causing a surge to run through her body. "I like you, Candace. A lot. And not as a friend. I wouldn't always be working with your company and I hope when that day comes, you'll allow me to be a part of your life."

Candace couldn't believe it. A week ago, she didn't think the opposite sex noticed her. Now here she was with a handsome man as he confessed his love for her.

"You don't have to say anything now. Let's just enjoy our time together." Marlon was an accurate representation of a gentleman, and the more time she spent with him, Candace was finding it harder to reject him. She held his gaze, her lips parting to speak, but then they were interrupted.

"Shrimp linguini for the man and my special zucchini lasagna for the lady. Bon appetite." Henry served them and turned left right away, sensing he was disturbing something. He had that connection with Marlon to sense his emotions. And at that moment, Marlon's emotions were intense.

After Henry left, Marlon changed the subject, focusing more on Candace's pleasurable pastimes. He found out she loved to read and watch Asian dramas even though she didn't speak any of the Asian languages. He told her about his childhood and traveling around the world and she laughed heartedly as he relayed his experience in the Amazon rainforest.

"I swear I thought I would die." The smile was in his eyes.

Candace had forgotten all her troubles, sinking into the magical night. "So, what did you do?"

"I dropped my stuff and hot-tailed it out of there as fast as I could." Marlon used his hands to display his fast motion. "I don't mess with anacondas. That's where I draw the line."

Candace held her stomach. She was laughing so hard that it was hard for her to maintain her composure. When she finally settled down, she said. "This is the most fun I've had in a long time."

Her words caused Marlon to straighten his face. "It doesn't have to end right now." He held her gaze. "How about we go to one more place tonight?"

Before, Candace would have objected. She would have made some excuse to reject Marlon's suggestion, but now that she had gotten to know him a lot better, there was only one thing to say. "Sure."

Chapter 7

Candace followed Marlon as he walked down the street, making a sudden stop as he slowed in front of the building.

"Is this where you want to go?" Her eyes dart up towards the sign, a sign she barely glimpsed when she sprinted away earlier that morning.

"It is," Marlon said, and then turned his body to get a better view of her, flinching as he noticed her growing paler. Marlon went forward and took her hand, his face stern and encouraging. "I'll be with you the entire time."

Candace took a step back, but something prevented her from completely retreating. She did not want Marlon to know what happened there the night before, but the look in Marlon's eyes reassured her everything was going to be fine.

Marlon held her hand and guided her into the bar just as the last group of patrons left.

Candace was hoping there would be other people and she could somehow blend into the crowd, but with the place empty, Paul's eyes fell on her easily.

Marlon made introductions. "Paul. This is the woman I was telling you about. Her name is—"

"Candace," Paul said, keeping his eyes on the woman that left his bed early in the morning. "We've met."

Candace turned away her head just as the two men shared a look.

"Candace, this is my bud, Paul. He owns this bar."

She tried to speak, but as hard as she tried, no sound came out, so she forced a smile and nodded instead.

Then Paul took her hand, his free one gently brushing the hair behind her ears. "Candace it's ok. Paul is irresistible to women. I understand."

Paul came closer to them, a smirk on his face and drinks in his hands. He shared it among the three and Candace reluctantly drank. By the time she was halfway through the glass, the effects of the alcohol were already prevalent. She was more relaxed and laughing at the duo's jokes. Just like Marlon, Paul had many interesting stories to tell. Stories she would have heard if she stuck around after they had sex.

"So, which one of us do you like more?" The question was unexpected, and Paul's expression told Candace he was serious.

She couldn't answer. Paul was tough and exciting, whereas Marlon was compassionate and gentle. They each had the qualities the others lacked. How did these two men become friends?

Candace's eyes were building now, her heart beating fast, until Marlon leaned over and placed his mouth on her lips. His kiss was gentle, and it renewed her spirit. She returned his kiss, closing her eyes in the moment. When Marlon pulled away, he said. "If you can't decide, you don't have to choose."

Candace tilted her head in confusion. What did Marlon mean by that? She didn't get to ask as Paul soon answered her. His act was similar to Marlon's but his kiss was much more domineering.

A concession of blinks followed as Candace tried to get a grasp on the situation.

"You could have us both if you want," Paul said, right before he placed another kiss on her lips. He deepened it, lifting her into his arms and carrying her away. Candace latched onto him, her feet around his waist.

Paul's release of her body onto the bed was far from gentle, but Marlon balanced his aggressiveness. He towered over her now, caressing every part of her body before his hand slid underneath her dress.

When he touched her, Candace's eyes rolled back, and she clung to the sheet. She was enjoying the intense sensation that came with Marlon's advances, and then he was gone. In his place, Paul removed the rest of her clothing, nipping her lip the entire time.

Not until he settled between her thighs, did she notice he was naked, sexy in all his glory. Candace held on firmly to his waist as he entered her, much like the night before, quickly placing her in a seductive trance. She latched on to his back, digging her nails into his flesh, an act that didn't seem to phase him. When his movements became more rapid, Candace knew he was close to his end and aided him.

Breathless, Paul withdrew and Marlon filled his place, but he didn't enter her. He pulled Candace on top of him and kissed her passionately, brushing her cheeks gently with the tips of his finger. And so, the hectic atmosphere had turned docile.

Marlon and Candace clung together until she grew restless. She wanted him, all of him, so Candace ignored all her previous concerns and eased onto him, gyrating back and forth as she did. Their rotations were slow and systematic, every inch of them shivering with passion. When Candace fell from her height, she took Marlon down with her and the two clung together, eventually falling asleep in each other's arms.

Chapter 8

Candace woke to whispered voices in the arms of one of her lovers. She looked to Marlon. His lips curved into a gentle smile as he slept, but Paul was not in the apartment.

At first, she settled into Marlon's arms, but something was gnawing at her. The voices were aggressive, and Paul's absence left her on edge.

She followed the voices as they led her to the bar, which was occupied by three bulky men. Paul was one of them, and he flinched as she approached.

"I did not realize that your taste in women has changed." Candace's eyes followed the words to a recognizable face. It was the man she ran into the night before. But it wasn't him who spoke. It was the skinnier one standing next to him. "I didn't realize you were into humans now?"

Human? What did he mean by that?

Candace found his comment strange but dismissed it as a misunderstanding. It had to be some inside joke implying Paul was a beast. After having sex with him twice, she could see how something like that could stick to him.

"I told you he had a human in here," the other one said to his companion, then directed his words to Paul. "You know better than to hoard the tributes. We share all with our tribe."

"You are mistaken." Paul's hand was folded into a fist, leaving the veins on his arms visible. "She is no tribute."

The men were staring at her now as if she was the only morsel in the lion's den. It made her uncomfortable, and she folded her arms and shifted her weight on one leg.

"Isn't she for the tribe?" The skinnier man's eyebrows were lifted, and he seem baffled that Paul was not offering her to them.

What was she anyway, some kind of object that could be tossed around and given away? Why were they speaking about her as if she had no authority over where she needed to be?

"I am not going anywhere with you, so you can get that silly thought out of your head." Candace suddenly felt invincible.

The bigger man laughed. "You seem to think that you have a choice in the matter." Then he became more serious. "Human mates are property of the tribe."

"I am no one's property," Candace shouted, placing her hands on her hips.

The bulky man laughed, and the other one narrowed his gaze at her. "You will return with us to our den, whether you like it or not." His gaze was intense, and it made her shiver.

"She's not going anywhere with you." Candace did not realize Marlon had entered the room. He walked in further, his eyes glowing green as he passed her. "I thought we made it clear that we are no longer part of the tribe."

"What do you feel this is? You can't just leave as you want. Our blood is not so easily discarded." The tension in the air was thick with the two intruders displaying as much aggression as her lovers. Still, Candace couldn't understand most of what they were saying.

"We're done following the bidding of the tribe blindly." Paul's veins were bulging now, and they also appeared to be pulsing. "From now on, we're following our own rules."

Paul's mysterious nighttime guest's hands were large, but at that moment they seemed larger. Unusually so. It looked as if it was outweighing his body.

Candace took a good look at the men. Both of them looked out of proportion, swelling on the face and the upper body. Taking a step backward, she looked at Marlon and Paul to realize that they had taken on a similar appearance.

The four men's bodies warped in and out of shape until they discarded their clothes and their human forms. Long nose replaced their short ones, and their eyes appeared more animalistic. Even the unique green eyes of her lovers adapted to their bodies' change, glowing in the darkness.

Candace's hand was clamped onto her mouth as she took in the full extent of their transformation: pointed ears, a protruding nose, large paws, fur, and hind legs. There was no doubt in her mind that these men were wolves.

No. Werewolves.

Candace shrieked as the biggest of them all leaped into the air and targeted the gray wolf, still trailing a piece of Paul's clothing. Based on its size, one hit from this wolf could cause serious injury. Luckily, it was slow, giving Paul enough time to jump out of the way and maneuver into an attack of his own.

Paul's wolf was swift, but not as much as Marlon's who battled the last wolf. They attacked each other with their paws, slashing across each other's faces and leaping into the air.

Tables and chairs tumbled to the floor as the fight escalated, leaving Candace shivering in the corner of the room. She had no idea what to do in that situation. Should she run or stay? Call the police or leave them to settle it? They were, after all, wolves. Would they even want the police involved?

In the end, Candace did nothing, her body unable to coordinate, especially with her indecisive thoughts. Instead, she squeezed herself into the corner and waited until the commotion ended. Until both Marlon had his opponent pinned down and Paul's was knocked out on the floor. Only then she could breathe again, but now she had a new problem. With the adrenaline rush normalizing, her brain now had time to accept what had happened.

She had two lovers, who were friends, and both turned into wolves. Not only this, but two other wolves were trying to claim her. It was an unbelievable reality, and its acceptance sent her into darkness.

Chapter 9

"Ugh." The sound spilled out of Candace's mouth before she opened her eyes. Pressing her hand against her forehead, she tried to ease herself off the bed.

A hand rested firmly on her shoulders, pushing her back down. "Take it easy. You were out of it for a while."

Candace forced herself to focus on the figure hovering above her, taking in his shrunken eyes and twisted mouth.

"Marlon," she whispered through dry lips. "I had the weirdest dream."

"Did you?" he asked before easing himself away. When Marlon returned, there was a glass of water in her hand and he clung to it while he assisted her in drinking. Then he settled her back in bed, snuggling her with the sheets. Finally, he released a heavy sigh but said nothing.

Still, Candace's dream disturbed her, and she felt the need to speak about it. "I dreamed that you, Paul, and two other men changed into wolves and had a big fight in the bar." She chuckled. "Isn't that ridiculous?"

Marlon looked at Paul, and the two exchanged a look before he tucked Candace in the sheet again, although nothing was out of place.

"Candace," Marlon said so softly she almost didn't hear him. "That was not a dream." He gave her a few seconds to digest the statement as Paul watched their interaction from across the room, leaning against the wall.

Candace's thoughts were still in shambles, so she believed she misheard him. "What?" She rubbed her temples in a circular motion to tried and relieve to pain in her head.

Marlon took a deep breath and released it. "Paul and I are werewolves. What you saw wasn't a dream. We really did turn into wolves."

Candace's eyes bulged and her jaw dropped slightly right before her lips began to quiver.

"You have nothing to fear. Paul and I will never hurt you." He paused. "We don't hurt anyone."

"And those guys," she stammered, her hand clutching the sheet.

"They are also werewolves." He took a deep breath and then went on to explain further. "Werewolves are pack creatures. We do and share everything."

"And follow our clan leader blindly," Paul said for the first time since Candace woke up. He said the words with so much scorn, like it was the thing he hated most in the world.

"That we do," Marlon agreed. "Or at least we used to. Paul and I grew tired of being someone's puppet and decided to leave the clan. The leader respected our decision. He doesn't want to force that life on anyone who doesn't want it. But some of the other members are not so understanding."

"We sent them back with their tail between their legs though," Paul joked, a smile plastered across his face.

Marlon took back control in explaining the situation the best he could, so as to not frighten Candace. "And don't worry. They won't bother us again. If they acted without the leader's consent - which I think they did - they would be punished for it."

"So they're gone?" she asked, her eyes searching the room.

"Yes. You don't have to worry about them," Marlon reassured her, cautiously tapping her hand. When he was confident enough, she wouldn't flinch from his touch, he took her hand in his completely, gently stroking it.

"What were those guys talking about when they mentioned tribute?" Candace was still a bit confused and while she had them in the explaining mood, she wanted to get as much information as she could.

"As a rule in our clan, if one of us takes a human mate, we are obligated to share her with the clan. You see, unlike humans, we have many mates." Marlon tapped her hand. "You don't have to be concerned about that. We will never share you with any of them."

Candace sighed, a soft smile framing her lips. "So what now?" she asked, looking from one man to the other.

"Well, that is completely up to you. You need to decide if you want to be part of our world or not," Paul said, his hand folded loosely across his chest. It was hard to determine how anxious he felt. Only his tightly pressed lips gave it away.

Candace hesitated. "Well, I don't know." She looked at both men. "Paul, you're tough and aggressively sexy and Marlon, you're compassionate and passionate. I have feelings for both of you." She lowered her head. "I'm sorry. I don't know who to choose."

"Who said you have to choose?" Marlon's words caused her head to rise again. "Did you not hear me say we share our human mates? Paul and I may not be in the clan anymore, but we are still brothers of the wolf. There are certain rules we still follow. What we want to know from you is if you would accept us as your mates. Do you object to being with werewolves?"

Candace didn't know how to answer that. Never in her years did she imagine having such a question thrown at her, so she didn't answer. At least not with words at first. She reached over and pressed her lips to Marlon's, noticing the immediate rise in his pants. When she pulled away, she said, "I don't think I can be with werewolves." Then a smile broadened across her face. "Luckily, to me, you guys are just Marlon and Paul, and my love for you will never fade."

THE END

Description

Aaron Locke is the 30 year old handsome CEO of Locke industries, worth billions of dollars. He is known as a chronic womanizer but he has a scandalous secret which he has guarded all his life. He finds himself attracted to Arabella, his P.A only to find out that she's the wife of his gay lover.

Arabella Garcia is a 28-year-old beautiful and curvy bear-shifter who is married to her childhood best-friend in order to hide his sexuality. She receives the shock of her life when she finds her husband cheating on her with her crush.

Bernard Garcia is a 32-year-old bear-shifter who was forced by his parents to marry his childhood best-friend Arabella. He finally finds the love of his life in Aaron.

Will Bernard be willing to share his love with Ara and will Ara be able to forgive the two men she holds dear to her heart?

Chapter 1

"Ara," Aaron called as he tapped Ara bringing her back to reality.

"We are here," Aaron stated looking at Arabella in concern.

Ara turned to look outside the window and noticed that his car was actually packed in front of the restaurant.

"I'm so sorry," Ara apologized for the tenth time that day. Mentally slapping herself for being absent minded and embarrassing herself in front of her boss again.

Aaron frowned knowing fully well that something was bothering her but decided not to probe further. He would bring that up later.

"'It's ok," he said as he leaned over and removed her seat belt keeping an eye on her as he did so.

Her heart fluttered as she got lost in his forest green eyes.

"Get down, Ara." He withdrew away from her and smiled, satisfied that he had such an effect on her.

"Yeah." She clumsily got out of the car feeling stupid for having been caught staring.

He led the way into the restaurant while she followed.

"Good evening, Mr. Locke." A tall blonde woman dressed in a waitress uniform greeted him.

He smiled flashing his perfect white teeth which made her blush.

"Please follow me to your private booth," said the Waitress.

"Ok," Aaron replied smiling at the woman who was clearly flirting with him.

Any other day he would have had his way with her but he couldn't afford to flirt back especially with Ara there. It just wasn't right.

They were led to the private booth while Aaron thanked the waitress who slipped a paper into his hand which most probably contained her number.

"What would you like to order?" the waitress asked her eyes fixed on Aaron.

It didn't skip Ara's attention that the Waitress had not acknowledged her for one second. She was too engrossed in flirting with Aaron to notice her.

Arabella rolled her eyes at the scene in front of her though it didn't come as a surprise to her.

Aaron was hot and handsome. He always made it to the list of the most sought after bachelors in America who had girls flaunting themselves at him.

He could get any girl at the snap of his finger but she always wondered why he couldn't just settle with one.

Aaron scanned the Restaurant's Menu for a few seconds before placing it back on the table.

"Get me an oven roasted Gulf fish fisherman's style with red wine."

"What about you, Ara?"

Ara forced a smile. "I will take the same order as yours."

She was not hungry. She just didn't want Aaron to ask her more questions.

"Ok," the waitress nodded, still not taking her eyes off Aaron who was beginning to look uncomfortable. She winked at him and wiggled her hips as she walked by, hoping he was watching her.

However, his eyes were fixed on Ara who was trying to stifle a laugh.

"What's funny?" he asked a hint of a smile on his face.

She looked so adorable trying not to laugh and he really wanted to know the reason behind her laughter. So he can do it again just to see her face light up.

"I'm just laughing at her antics. She is willing to lose her job for you and you didn't even spare her a glance."

"How could I when I have someone more precious in front of me?" he blurted out but didn't regret it on seeing her blush and shift on her chair.

She looked around the private booth hoping for a distraction to calm her nerves. She looked back at him only to find his gaze still on her.

She cleared her throat in an attempt to ease the tension and asked "When is the Client going to get here?"

He started chuckling.

"What did I say that is so funny?" Ara thought.

"Why are you laughing, sir?"

He stops chuckling and leaned on the table, his gaze now serious.

"I've told you countless times that you shouldn't call me sir outside the office."

Ara bit her lip. "I'm sorry, Aaron."

"Good." He smiled, satisfied by her answer.

"You still haven't answered my question. Where is the client that we are supposed to meet here?"

He starts chuckling again and shook his head. "Oh! Ara, you are so innocent."

"There's no client. I brought you here so we could talk."

She opened her mouth in shock and closed it back "Why?"

"I have noticed that you have been distracted at work lately. I keep on asking you what's wrong but you keep evading the subject."

Ara rolled her eyes, offended that he had tricked her. "That's because I don't want to talk about it."

He sighed and clasped his hands together.

" Ara, I thought we'd passed this stage. I confided in you about my personal issues something I've never done before. I thought we are friends."

Ara sighed. "Yes, we are."

"Then what is stopping you from confiding in me, your friend?"

Seeing that she remained silent, he continued.

"I respect your choice but I can see that there's something eating you up and you really need to vent it out. Mind you I'm a good listener." He flashed his pearly white teeth.

Ara shook her head in disapproval. "I can't tell you. It's not appropriate."

"Is it about your husband?" he asked, catching her off guard. The look on her face and the fact that she made no effort to deny it confirmed Aaron's suspicions.

"How... how did you know? Is it that obvious?" Ara asked.

"I have my ways but that's not important right now."

He placed his hand on hers.

"Talk to me, your secret is safe with me."

"It's not that important." Ara dismissed. She wasn't used to being vulnerable especially in front of her Boss.

He rolled his eyes at her and crossed his arms. "It's important enough for you to be distracted at work and end up spilling hot coffee all over me."

She bit her lip recalling the mistake she had made earlier that day at the office.

She had been filling his cup with coffee but was lost in thoughts that she didn't notice that the cup was full until Aaron shouted and she saw that it had stained his suit.

"I told you to see me as your friend outside the company. You can trust me with that. Like I said your secret is safe with me." He assured placing his hand on yours.

She sighed knowing he was right. She really needed someone to confide in but she had no friends here. All her relatives were still primitive preferring not to mingle with humans. She also couldn't confide in them without being judged.

"It's just... I don't know... it might not be true... I just feel like my husband is cheating on me."

"What? Why would you think that?" he asked in surprise. He clearly wasn't expecting that.

"I've been seeing the signs and a lady is 80-percent right when she suspects that her man is cheating on her."

"But you can't be so sure."

"I know but I just can't help feeling this way," Ara muttered sadly.

His heart hurt seeing her so vulnerable. He squeezed her hand softly making her look up at him.

"If he's really cheating on you then he's nothing but a loser."

"You are an impeccable woman, Ara, any man would be lucky to have you."

"Nah, you are just saying that just to make me feel better." Ara dismissed smiling.

He lifted her hand up and kissed it affectionately keeping his eyes on her.

"I meant every word."

Her heart fluttered at the gesture and she wondered how his lips would feel on hers.

As soon as the thought appeared, she quickly withdrew her hand away from his, wondering why she had such improper thoughts about him.

Though, she couldn't blame herself entirely. He was every woman's dream and her secret crush but he didn't have to know that.

It was wrong, totally wrong to feel that way about him as a married woman but she couldn't help it. That's why she always minimized their physical contacts, afraid that she would fall in deep with no going back.

She cleared her throat in order to get rid of the awkwardness in the air.

It was then the waitress arrived with their orders.

Ara had never been so happy to see the waitress again. She had saved her from the obvious tension in the room.

The waitress left after delivering their orders.

Ara cleared his throat once again. "We should probably start eating."

"Yeah, you are right," said Aaron his eyes never leaving Ara.

They ate their food in silence each of them wondering how to break the awkwardness in the air.

He was getting irritated with the silence.

"I'm sorry for making you uncomfortable," Aaron apologized while Ara looked up from her meal and smiled.

"You didn't."

"I clearly did." He watched her lips as she ate.

A little stain was by her lips and he wondered how it would feel to brush his fingers against her lips.

Feeling his gaze on her, she looked up from her meal.

"Ara, you got a little uh- something here." He gestured to her lip.

"Oh!" she muttered and licked the side of her lip.

"Damn, she would be the death of me." He thought as he watched her try to lick the stain off with no idea what it was doing to him.

"Is it gone?" she innocently asked a flustered Aaron.

Aaron shook his head and she groaned. He sighed and left his seat to sit beside her.

Ara's heart quickened at the proximity. She couldn't stand being close to him with those forest green eyes boring into her brown orbs.

"Here," he said as he brought his thumb to the side of her upper lip, his hand slightly gracing her lips.

He marveled at how soft they were and with just a wipe, the stain was gone but his thumb stayed put and his eyes stayed glued on her lips wondering how it would feel to kiss them.

He looked up to meet her eye but found them staring at his lips with as much longing as his own. He needed no further clue to know that she wanted this as much as him.

Her eyes stayed glued to his lips watching as his tongue darted out to wet pink lips.

Her eyes snapped up immediately hoping that she hadn't been caught but the look in his eyes told her that she had been caught.

Before she could bring herself to say something, Aaron had planted her lips on her.

He kissed her sweetly and softly before he pulled away to meet her gaze.

His heart was beating frantically against his chest. He so bad wanted to kiss her again but he needed to know that she wanted it as much as him.

"Ara," he whispered bringing her back to reality.

"Yes?" she managed to say hoping that she didn't sound too nervous.

"Was that... was that ok? Can I kiss you again?" he asked slowly hoping that he had not scared her away.

She didn't know what did it for her. Was it the look of hope in his eyes or the fact that she wanted to kiss him again?

The next thing she knew, she had kissed him.

He froze in shock at her action but quickly recovered and kissed her back harder. She reached up and wrapped her hands around the back of his neck pulling him closer.

Butterflies exploded in her chest as he slipped his tongue into her mouth relishing in the taste of her. She moaned when she felt his hand grip her hips.

He needed to have her closer to him. No woman had made him hard with just a kiss.

He had kissed so many girls before her but they paled in comparison.

He was dying to have her close and bury himself in her. Having her scream his name all night as he fucked her senseless.

She gasped as he felt his hand move to her open thigh rubbing slowly. Then her eyes snapped open bringing her back to reality.

She was kissing her boss. She was kissing Aaron in the restaurant. She was kissing another man when she was a married woman. She was a married woman!

She quickly pushed him away as reality dawned on her.

He nearly whined as she broke the kiss but stopped on seeing the look on her face.

Her eyes were watery as if on the verge of tears. Her hand moved to cover her swollen lips as she stifled a cry.

He tried to reach for her but she stood up shaking her head. "Don't touch me!" she managed to say her voice breaking.

She quickly grabbed her purse and ran out of the restaurant.

"Shit," Aaron cursed as he ran after her.

He found her on the street waving various cabs down as they passed. He brushed his hand through his hair and walked to her, grabbing her hand to make her face him.

"Don't touch me!" she yelled this time.

"Ara, I'm sorry," he apologized sincerely. He shouldn't have put her in a vulnerable position. He was sorry for that but he wasn't sorry for kissing her.

He would give anything to kiss those lips again but it wasn't right. She was a married woman and he had to respect that.

"I'm really sorry."

"No, you are not. You clearly wanted it."

He ran his hands through his hair again wondering what to say to her.

"This shouldn't have happened. It should never have happened. This is all my fault. I shouldn't have followed you to this stupid dinner. I shouldn't have allowed you to take advantage of me."

He frowned not believing his ears. "I took advantage of you?"

He let out a laugh devoid of humour "You clearly wanted it. I asked for your consent and what did you do, you kissed me back."

Her heart sank as she took in his words. He was right. She had entertained him. It was her fault. She was the married one. She should have had more control over her feelings.

"Just leave me alone." She pleaded eager to leave the premises. The close proximity between them was not helping her mental state at the moment.

He gave her an incredulous look. "I can't just leave you alone in the middle of nowhere."

"Yes, you can. Now please let me go."

She looked down at his hold on her arm but he didn't budge.

"No, let me drive you home." He protested ignoring her plea.

"Are you crazy? Do you really expect me to let you drive me home after what happened between us?"

He knew she was right but he couldn't just leave her all by herself.

"Please leave me alone. I'm begging you," she pleaded.

The desperation in her voice tugged at his heart and he let her go.

He walked back to where his car was parked and waited until she got inside a cab.

He really wanted to follow her home but he realised how foolish that would be. He had done enough damage already.

Chapter 2

She paused on her way to the front door when she spotted her husband's car in the garage.

He's home early. She thought to herself.

Normally, she would be happy because it was a rare occurrence for him to be home before her but the guilt in her wasn't eager to see him just yet.

She felt like a hypocrite for suspecting him to be cheating when she was doing the same.

Her hand reached for the doorknob and she sighed.

She mustered up courage and opened the door confirming her suspicions.

There he was seated on the sofa in the living room watching the news when his eyes met hers as she entered.

His face broke into a wide grin as he jumped out of the sofa and rushed towards her, enveloping her in an embrace.

She froze at his sudden action wondering why he was so happy.

Bernard frowned when Ara refused to hug him back. He slowly released her from his embrace to look at her.

"What's wrong?" he asked brushing a strand of hair that was blocking her vision away.

She finally managed to find her voice. "Good evening, Darling." She greeted while he just gave her a questioning look.

"That doesn't answer my question."

She shrugged out of his hold and made her way to the kitchen.

Afraid that he would see right through her after all, he was her best-friend. He knew everything about her.

"Nothing is wrong with me," she answered as she opened the fridge and took out a chilled bottled water and downed the contents into a glass cup.

"Are you sure? You don't look fine to me," he asked worriedly.

She looked to be hiding something from him and it scared him because Ara never hid any secrets from him. He was her confidante.

Yeah right. You don't want her to hide things from you but you are doing the same to her, his subconscious said to him making him feel guilty and brush the thought way.

"I said I'm fine!" she snapped startling him.

She looked up to meet his gaze. He looked offended and she couldn't blame him.

She brought the cup to her lips and sipped her water in order to calm her nerves.

"Why are you home late?" he asked all of a sudden as he made his way to the kitchen to stand beside her.

She almost spat out the water she was drinking at his question.

Feeling his gaze on her, she placed the cup back on the kitchen cabinet and took a deep breath before she answered.

"I was at a business meeting with my boss." Technically she wasn't lying. She really thought it would be a business meeting until Aaron told her the truth.

"A business meeting where you kiss your boss," her subconscious asked her making her guilt to return ten folds.

"I... I have to freshen up. Good night." She smiled at him and scurried off to the bathroom to avoid his questioning gaze.

Bernard leaned against the kitchen cabinet as he watched her leave for their room.

He couldn't blame her for acting cold to him when he had been doing the exact same thing for the past for four months.

He took a sip from her abandoned cup and sighed.

Ever since he had met Aaron at the pub, he had been complete.

They had hooked up and at first he thought what he felt for him was just a fluke but when he couldn't help going back to him, he knew it wasn't just a fluke.

He had found his soulmate.

His bear purred every time he saw Aaron. He sighed as felt himself harden at the thought of Aaron.

All his life, he had been nothing but a good son to his parents even to the point of hiding his sexuality because it wasn't acceptable for bear-shifters to be gay. They were supposed to end up with their soul-mate, a female bear-shifter.

He didn't mean to cheat on Ara but theirs was not a normal marriage. Gay bears were an abomination and she saved his family reputation by marrying him.

She had always been in love with him since they were kids but he couldn't return that love no matter how much he tried to. He just couldn't do it.

He loved her but he was not in love with her.

How would he break it to her that he had defiled their marriage vows? She deserved to know but he couldn't bear to break her heart. She was too dear to him.

He made his way into their room and sat down on the bed. There was no going back. He would tell her the truth now. No matter how hard it would be. She deserved to know.

He heard the sound of the shower stopping and her footsteps as she made her way into the room wrapped in a white robe.

She gasped in shock on seeing him there.

"Bernard?"

He smiled at her. "I figured that it's time for me to retire to bed too."

He gestured to her to sit on his laps while she looked at him in question.

"Please."

She sighed and sat on his laps wrapping her hands round his neck while he rocked her back and forth as if she was a baby.

"I'm sorry," he muttered while she looked at him confused.

"I'm sorry for the way I've been acting for the past few months. I shouldn't have treated you coldly."

Ever since he had started cheating on her with Aaron, he had been cold to her just to hide his guilt.

She shook her head and placed her finger on his lip to cut him off.

"Shh... I should have been more understanding."

He shook his head not agreeing with her. "No you don't get it Ara, I... I..."

He groaned. *Why is it so hard to say?* he thought to himself.

"I-"

She cut him off and kissed him.

She moaned in pleasure as she explored his mouth. She needed him so bad.

She gripped the collar of his chest pulling him closer. She needed him so bad.

It's been so long since they had had sex. Exactly five months and she couldn't stand it anymore.

She grinded against him, making him groan against her mouth.

She stood up and let her robe slip off her body revealing her naked tanned curvy body. She climbed unto his lap again and whispered in his ear.

"Make love to me."

He froze and gently pushed her away.

"I can't. I can't do it."

She pulled away slightly to look at his face and frowned "You can't?"

He avoided her gaze. "Yes, I'm sorry."

"I'm just not in the mood. Let's just go back to sleep."

The disappointed look on her face told him he had messed up once again but how could he sleep with her when Aaron was on his mind. He couldn't sleep with her and risk moaning Aaron's name.

He couldn't do that to her. It was not fair to her.

She slowly got out of his lap, picked up her robe from the floor and wore it.

He reached for her hand. "Ara, I'm sorry."

"it's ok. It's fine." She didn't look at him. She was disappointed. He had rejected her once again.

She climbed onto bed and slipped the covers over her.

He knew it wasn't fine. She was mad at him. So mad!

He ran his hand through his blonde hair in frustration. He didn't know how he could make it up to her but he knew it was better if he left her alone for a while so he left for the guest room.

Chapter 3

She released a shaky breath as someone's fingers pushed in and out of her in an unrelenting tempo.

Pleasure built between her legs as they trembled causing her to release a soft moan.

"Faster." She gasped loudly arching her back wanting to feel the fingers inside her the more.

The person increased the pace, slamming his fingers in and out of her, circling her clit bringing her closer to her release.

Her panting ceased for a moment and she slowly opened her eyes to behold familiar forest green eyes staring down at her.

"Aaron?" she asked in shock.

He smirked. "The one and only."

He gave her one last thrust and she came all over his fingers.

"Ara."

She felt someone tap her.

"Ara."

Ara's eyes snapped open as she took in her surroundings. She sat up when she saw Bernard was staring down at her in concern.

"Are you ok?" he asked.

She managed to nod wiping the sweat on her forehead with her palm.

She had just had a wet dream about her boss, Aaron. It was a miracle that she didn't moan out his name. It would have been embarrassing.

"You are late for work."

She quickly glanced at the wall clock the memories of the kiss she shared with Aaron coming back to her like a vengeance.

No, I can't go to work. I just had a wet dream about him. How can I handle working with him when I can't even resist him? The right thing to do as a married woman is to resign and that's what I'm going to do. She thought to herself.

"My boss gave me a morning break because of the late night meeting we had yesterday," she lied.

She couldn't bring herself to tell him just yet that she was resigning because that would prompt a lot of questions that she wasn't ready to answer.

"Your boss is so nice," Bernard said as he fixed his apron.

If only you knew. She thought to herself.

"By the way, breakfast is ready. Should I bring it here or you will come down to eat?" he asked a flustered Ara.

"I will come down to eat it. Right now I need to freshen up." she replied wanting some time alone to herself to gather her thoughts.

He smiled and pecked her on the lips before leaving the room.

As soon as he left, she reached under the blanket to her night robe and felt her wetness.

She didn't just come in her dream but in real life too.

She scurried off the bed and headed for the bathroom in need for a cold shower. She would have to draft the resignation letter immediately for her own sanity.

Bernard removed his apron and placed it on the kitchen cabinet.

He brushed his hand through his hair as he remembered how Ara writhed on the bed.

He knew she had a wet dream especially after he denied her sex last night. He would have to make it up to her and look for a way to get Aaron out of his system.

It wasn't fair to Ara at all.

Chapter 4

Aaron was restless as he paced his office waiting for the one person he was dying to see.

He took a glance at his wristwatch which read 12:30 pm and groaned.

"How could she not report to work?" he asked himself as he loosened his tie. He threw the tie across the room not caring where it landed.

A knock came on the door and he yelled, "What?"

The door opened to reveal a gorgeous Arabella who was dressed in a black crew-neck sweater with a black leather mini dress which hugged her hourglass shape which made his mouth dry up.

"How dare she look so good? How am I supposed to keep my hands to myself with her dressed like this?" he thought to himself.

He shook his dirty thoughts away and frowned, "You are late."

He went back to his seat and sat down folding his arms trying to look like he was furious with her when it was the exact opposite.

He was going to act like the boss she wanted.

She didn't say anything. She just made her way to his table and handed him a white envelope.

He stared at the envelope in confusion.

"What is this?" he asked as he collected the envelope.

"That's my resignation letter."

"What!" he exclaimed in shock. He couldn't have possibly heard her right.

She rolled her eyes. "You heard me."

"Why are you resigning? It doesn't make sense."

He stood up and walked towards her.

"If this is about what happened last night, I'm sorry. It won't happen again."

"I admit I crossed my boundaries but please don't leave me." He pleaded.

The sincerity behind his words melted her heart and the fact that he was just few feet away from her didn't help matters.

The first two buttons of his white shirt were unbuttoned revealing smooth tan skin. His white shirt fitted him perfectly, hugging his abs.

She wondered how it would feel to run her hands over them. Then she remembered her dream, the way he was...

She felt herself getting wet at the memory.

"This is the right thing to do," she managed to say ignoring her improper thoughts.

He closed the space between them and traced his thumb from her cheek to her lips.

"But why does it feel so right?" he whispered, his hot breath fanning her face.

He didn't give her time to digest what was going on before he grabbed her neck, pulling her closer and kissing her.

It didn't take long for her to start to struggle against him but he didn't budge deepening the kiss.

She felt him moving her towards the table until her butt sat on it.

She couldn't resist anymore and she kissed him back with as much ferocity, brushing her hands through his hair.

His free hand started trailing up her slightly parted thighs until he reached her soaked panties. She was wet for him making him smirk.

His hand rubbed her wet pussy through her thong making her let out a soft moan.

He pulled out of the kiss and rested his forehead against hers "You are so wet for me." He smiled as his fingers pushed her thong out of the way rubbing her the more.

She threw her head back moaning. It's been so long since she had been touched like this. It had been so-so long so it was understandable that her body was betraying her.

Before she could make a final decision on whether she should follow her brain or not, he had already slipped his fingers into her wet cunt making her let out a loud moan, arching her back wanting him to push into her the more.

"Do you want this?" he asked as he withdrew his finger and pinched at her swollen clit, teasingly rubbing his fingers on her outer lips.

Her brain was telling her to push him away but her body stayed put letting him explore her secret haven.

"Yes," she whispered. It was barely a whisper but he heard her alright.

"Yes what?" he asked as he slipped one finger into her again circling it.

"Yes, I want it," she whimpered.

He smiled happy and pushed two more fingers into her making her cry out in pleasure.

He began to push his fingers in and out of her, thrusting into her harder and faster. He caught her whimpers with a deep kiss.

She was writhing against him and he could feel himself getting hard by her motion.

His cock was straining out of his trousers begging to be released. Damn, he wanted to fuck her on the table right there but he couldn't do it.

He didn't want their first time to be over the table. She was special. She was his Ara, not some random fling.

He sped up his swirls around her clit making her lean against him.

Not long after, she was climaxing, bucking hard as she cried out, squirting and cumming all over his fingers.

He withdrew his fingers slowly and licked it clean watching her.

It was then it dawned on her that she had just been fingered by another man other than her husband. She felt like a slut.

She quickly pulled her skirt down and walked away from him as if he was some plague.

"Oh my God, What have I done?" she asked herself.

He chuckled. "You mean what have we done?"

She rolled her eyes and glared at him.

"Hey, there's no need to feel bad. I mean we both wanted this. We are both adults who clearly wanted this."

"But this is wrong."

"Says the woman whose husband is probably somewhere fucking a bitch's brain out and you are here denying yourself pleasure."

"That still doesn't make what we did, right."

"The sooner you accept that you want me as much as I want you, the better for you cause if you think I'm going let you go, you must be joking."

She shook her head. "I'm not going to stand here and let you ruin my marriage, Goodbye forever, Mr. Locke."

She didn't spear him a second glance before she dashed out of his office banging the door after her.

He would be damned to let her go.

Ever since, she had walked into his into his office a year ago looking for work. He had been entranced with her.

He wanted to bed her bad but when he found out that she was married, he had to keep his feelings in check.

He didn't mess with married women but as he got to know her better, he realised that he wasn't just interested in sleeping with her, he wanted to be with her and the only person he had ever felt that way for was Bernard. How would Bernard take this news?

He felt his member harden at the thought of Bernard. He really needed him right now.

He picked up his phone from the table and dialed Bernard's number.

Chapter 5

Aaron parked his Tesla in front of Bernard's House and got out slamming the door after him.

He stood beside his car as he admired the modest house. He had always wondered why Bernard never wanted him to know where he lived.

Aaron had thought he was living in a rugged neighborhood but when the private investigator he hired had sent the pictures to him, it was then he knew there was something else Bernard was trying to hide from him.

He observed his surroundings for a while before he pressed the doorbell.

Bernard was in the kitchen washing the dishes when he heard the sound of the doorbell.

He frowned wondering who it could be since he wasn't expecting any visitor and neither was Ara after all she was visiting her Mum in Placerville and wouldn't be back till the next day.

He sighed and cleaned his hands with the hand towel, then headed for the front door. He hesitated a little and opened it only to receive the shock of his life.

There standing on the doorstep was Aaron, looking as handsome as ever in a casual white shirt and dark blue jeans matched with blue sneakers. Bernard gulped as he stared at the love of his life.

Aaron broke into a wide grin and held out his arms for a hug "Surprise."

Bernard looked behind Aaron in panic. "What are you doing here?"

Aaron smiled. "To see you." he said it as if it was the most obvious thing in the world.

"But you can't be here!"

Aaron closed the space between them pressing his chest against Bernard's own.

"Why not?" he whispered in his ear and bit it softly.

Bernard felt his cock start to harden in his pants but he ignored it and took a step back. He couldn't allow Aaron to enter into his house and find out he was married this way.

Aaron pushed Bernard out of the way and entered the room with Bernard following after.

"You have to leave now!" Bernard tried to appear firm ignoring Aaron's intense gaze.

"Do you really want me to leave?" Aaron asked as he gripped the back of Bernard's head and kissed him, grinding his hard length against his.

Bernard moaned kissing Aaron back passionately. He moaned in protest when Aaron pulled away.

"Take me to your room."

It was a command that he couldn't resist. He captured Aaron's lips devouring it like he couldn't let go as he led him down the hall way to his room.

They grabbed at each other's clothes till they were naked. Aaron laid Bernard on the bed, their tongues still exploring each other.

Aaron reached down and grabbed Bernard's cock stroking it, earning a groan from Bernard.

"I missed you," Aaron said as he squeezed Bernard's cock extra hard making him whimper.

They relished at the skin to skin contact, their cocks rubbing against each other. They continued to pump each other, groans and moans filling the room.

"I need you," whispered Bernard.

Aaron grinned and withdrew away from him.

"Lay face down," he commanded Bernard who eagerly obeyed after grabbing a jar of Vaseline on the bed side table and handed it to a pleased Aaron.

Aaron took a handful of the Vaseline and rubbed it all over his cock. He rubbed his hardened member on Bernard's butt, guiding his slippery cock towards his tight hole.

He placed the head of his thick cock to Bernard's hole and pushed in slowly till he could go no further.

"Harder," Bernard mumbled while Aaron retreated a little before thrusting in, harder and faster.

"You feel so damn good!" Aaron hissed, his voice almost lost in pleasure. He grabbed both of Bernard's hands with his own and laid his chest on his back as his cock slid in and out of the other man smoothly.

Aaron closed his eyes imagining Ara under him as he fucked her in different positions while she cries out his name.

He grunted as he increased his strokes, aggressively fucking the man under him.

"I'm gonna cum soon. Come on." Bernard growled.

"Oh god," moaned Aaron quickening his pace, even more.

The sound of a door creaking open made him freeze.

"Is there anybody else here?" he asked Bernard.

"No, it's probably the breeze. Just don't stop," he answered with his eyes closed in ecstasy.

"Cum!" he demanded increasing his pace even more, making Bernard let out a strangled moan and trembled shouting Aaron's name as he came, spurting onto the sheets below him.

Unable to hold it back any longer, Aaron gripped Bernard's palm and spilled his seeds into his ass.

Panting, he lay beside Bernard exhausted trying to catch his breath.

He stared at the spent man beside him and muttered, "I love you, Bernard."

He traced his fingers through his hair while Bernard whispered, "I love you too."

He was about to kiss Bernard when they heard a loud gasp and saw Ara leaning against the door.

Chapter 6

She brought her hand to her mouth at the scene in front of her. She had entered the house only to hear loud groans and moans.

She decided to check for herself only to see Aaron and her husband naked in an intimate position. It didn't take her too long to put two and two together and discover that they had sex.

Heartbroken and feeling betrayed, she ran out of the room to the parlor sinking to the floor as she tried to make sense of what she just saw.

"Shit!" Bernard cursed as he climbed out of bed and quickly slipped his boxers on.

"What is going on? Why is she here?"

"'She's my wife!" Bernard blurted out not bothering to hide the truth anymore.

"What!" Aaron was in shock as he sat up on the bed.

"Yeah, I have to go."

He didn't wait for Aaron's answer before he darted out of the room to see Ara on the floor staring into space.

He sat beside her and sighed.

"I know that there's nothing I'm going to say that would fix this but-"

She turned to look at him with tear-stricken eyes cutting him off. "I knew you were cheating on me. I was ok with it but I didn't expect it to be with my boss." Her voice broke as she tried to blink her tears away.

"I didn't know he was your boss until I had fallen deep. Believe me I didn't want to hurt you."

"But you did. You still did. You had the guts to do it on our matrimonial bed." She paused to catch her breath and continued. "How many times have you done this on that same bed that we sleep on? Don't you have any shame?"

"Listen, Ara, I didn't mean to... it just so happened that..."

"That what?" she snapped.

The sound of footsteps interrupted their conversation and they looked up just in time to see Aaron walk into the room fully dressed.

Ara stood up and stomped toward him, landing a slap on his face.

"How could you?"

Aaron rubbed his cheek and glanced towards Bernard who was avoiding his gaze in guilt.

"Ara!"

"Don't you dare call my name! Was this your plan all along? You were using me the same way you used him?"

"No, no, you are getting this all wrong. I didn't know he was your husband," Aaron tried to clarify to a fuming Ara.

"Óh! So you found out just now!"

"That's exactly what happened." He nodded hoping that she would believe him. He knew Bernard was hiding something. He just wasn't expecting it to be this. Why of all women did he have to be married to Ara.

She scoffed, rolling her eyes, not believing him one bit.

Bernard stood up and sighed. "He's right. I didn't tell him that I was married. Even when I found out that you worked for him, I still didn't tell him. And I'm sorry for that, Aaron. I'm really sorry." He apologized looking down at the floor with red cheeks.

Ara ran her hands through her hair and exhaled "How long has this been going on?" she asked no one in particular.

"Four... four months," Bryan stammered knowing now that she was never going to forgive him. He had been distant to her for those four months.

She closed her eyes and asked the question that had been plaguing her mind since she caught them in the act. "Do you love him?"

He hesitated a little wondering how he could lessen the hurt she was going through because of him but he knew he had already hurt her enough. There was no going back from here.

"Yes, I love him."

Her heart broke at his confession. Bernard was her first everything, her first love, the first man who made love to her. The only man she had sworn that she would ever love.

It was hard to grasp that he was in love with someone else, not just someone else but her boss, the same person she was starting to fall for.

Unable to stand the tension in the room and wanting some alone time to himself to understand the situation, Aaron announced.

"I will just go." He didn't wait for any answer. He made to leave but Ara held his hand preventing him from leaving.

He turned to look at her.

"Nobody is leaving here until we settle this," she said with an air of finality looking at the two men in front of her.

She turned to look at Aaron who had a questioning look on his face and asked, "Do you love him too?"

He wasn't expecting that question at all. Neither did she expect that she would stop him from leaving. He looked at Bernard who was already staring at him in anticipation waiting for him to admit the truth.

"I do," he finally replied avoiding Ara's gaze.

She suddenly started clapping and let out a laugh devoid of humor. "Bravo, the great Aaron Locke is in love. Let's see how long that would last."

She moved to stand beside Bernard who was already feeling anxious wondering what she was up to.

"Bernard, why don't you show your love who you really are? Don't you want to see if he really loves you?"

He could sense the mockery in her voice. He refused to believe she was suggesting that. She couldn't possibly be suggesting what he thought she was suggesting.

"I don't know what you are talking about." He prayed that his suspicions wouldn't come true.

She scoffed "Oh! Please Bernard, aren't you tired of the lies? Don't you want to know if his feelings are true?"

Aaron frowned obviously confused. "'What is going on here?"

"Good question," Ara smiled. "Bernard here has one more secret he is hiding from you."

Aaron turned his gaze to an anxious looking Bernard. "Bernard, is this true?"

Bernard remained silent wishing that the ground would just swallow him up right there.

"He won't be able to tell you but I will show you."

She reached behind her back and zipped down her dress and slipped out of it.

Aaron's confused gaze turned to that of shock as he took in her appearance. She was now semi-naked with a pink c-cup bra and matching lace panties.

He could see through her panties that she was totally bare. He felt himself harden at the mesmerizing sight in front of him.

He closed his eyes and shook his head willing the image away. This was not the right time.

"What the hell are you doing?" Bernard asked Ara who rolled her eyes.

"What you should have done a long time ago before you got yourself in this mess."

Then she shifted into a gorgeous brown bear with red highlights, startling Aaron who took several steps back in disbelief until his back hit the wall.

"What...what is going on here?" he asked a Bewildered Bernard who was still finding it hard to believe that Ara had just shifted in front of Aaron.

"What the hell is that thing?" he asked again pointing to the brown bear whose eyes were fixed on him.

"That's Ara."

Aaron's eyes widened as he took in the information. That couldn't be Ara. It wasn't possible. Yes, she was right there before this thing came out. It just couldn't be.

"She's a werebear, so am I." Bernard finally admitted changing into a brown bear as well.

"This has to be a dream. You must be kidding me."

Aaron felt dizzy as if he was about to faint.

Unable to handle the scene in front of him, he rushed out of the room.

He ran till he got to his car panting as he leaned against it.

"I must be going crazy," he said to himself as he tried to catch his breath. "This can't be real."

He managed to enter his car and leaned back against his chair trying to make sense of what he had just witnessed.

"Aaron, let me explain." Bernard shouted as he ran towards Aaron's car in his boxers.

Aaron eyes widened and he turned the car on ignoring Bernard.

"Aaron!" Bernard called.

"Don't you dare mention my name again, you sick lunatic." Aaron said rolling up the car window to blur Bernard's words.

“If you don't want to die yet, get the fuck away from my car.”

He started moving the car in warning while Bernard stepped back and watched as Aaron zoomed off.

Chapter 7

Ara sipped her coffee staring into space. It had been two weeks since she had sent Bernard out of the house and she hadn't heard from him. She couldn't blame him especially with the way she acted towards him that last time.

***

Bernard was still staring at Aaron's retreating car only to turn back when he heard a screeching sound.

Ara was dragging his luggage with her and when she saw him, she threw it at him.

It landed beside him with some of his clothes flying out and laying scattered on the floor.

"What is the meaning of this?" asked a Bewildered Aaron.

"I'm setting you free. You are now free to go back to your lover."

"You don't know what you are doing. You are not even thinking."

"How could you shift in front of him? How could you?" He was furious now.

"What about you? Were you thinking before you slept with a human? You know it's against the rules but you still did it."

"So by shifting in front of him, what were you planning to achieve?"

"I've achieved my aim. Let's see if he would want to have anything to do with you now."

He shook his head at her. "You are obviously not in your right senses so I'm going to leave you alone but I will be back."

***

Maybe she had overreacted but she couldn't blame herself totally. After seeing the scene in front of her that day, she couldn't think clearly and vented her anger the wrong way.

The doorbell rang interrupting her thoughts.

That must be Bernard. she thought as she placed her coffee on the table. He had texted her an hour ago that he was on his way to pick his things.

"Come in, the door is not locked."

The door opened to reveal a tired looking Bernard. His eyes were puffy as if he had been having a tough time sleeping.

"Are you ok?" she couldn't help but ask.

"What do you think?"

"Hey, don't give me an attitude," she warned.

"Or what? You have already done your worst. I've lost Aaron. He doesn't want to have anything to do with me. I haven't seen or heard from him in two weeks. Two weeks! Hope you are happy now?"

"Well don't blame me for trying to knock some sense into you." She was now standing up with her arms folded glaring at him.

"And why are you so mad? Is it because I cheated on you or because you just can't accept that the men you love don't want you?"

Her mouth hanged open in shock "What... what are you insinuating?"

He scoffed. "I'm not insinuating anything. He told me about your little romp in his office."

Seeing that she was confused, he continued, "I knew about his little crush on you, I just didn't know that you felt the same until he told me about what you guys did in his office. I must admit it did turn me on when he told me about it."

He bit his lip on realising that he was being harsh on her.

"Ara," he called softly. "I know I wronged you. I really did hurt you but believe me when I say I didn't want to hurt you."

"I couldn't bring myself to tell you that I was in love with Aaron because I knew how much you loved me. I tried to break it off with him that was why he looked for me and came here," he explained.

She sighed. "I'm sorry for overreacting. I shouldn't have acted the way I did."

"No." Bernard shook his head. "You had every right to react that way."

"No I don't. I always told you that I would support you when you find your soul-mate but what did I do, I acted like a jealous lunatic and sent you away."

She closed the space between them and asked. "Do you miss him?"

Bernard closed his eyes and smiled. "I do. I miss him so much," he replied.

"I miss him, too," she confessed while he opened his eyes in surprise.

"I didn't plan on falling in love with him. It just happened that's why I resigned because I couldn't resist him. I feared that if I worked for him any longer I would cheat on you," she explained.

He cupped her cheeks. "You did the right thing which I failed to do."

"Shh..." she shushed him. "What would happen to us now?" she asked.

"It's left for you to decide."

She leaned her forehead against his. "I don't want to divorce you. I can't bring myself to let you go. Call me selfish but I can't."

"Then don't," he answered.

She gave him a questioning look. "What do you mean?"

"I totally understand. I get it. I don't want a divorce either."

"But what about Aaron?"

"As you can see he couldn't handle the truth and left me."

She looked away from him feeling guilty. She had let her anger get the best of her and now he was heartbroken.

"Let me make it up to you." She pressed her lips to his and he wrapped his hands around her waist pulling her closer. Her hands trailed down his chest to his groin and she rubbed him through his jeans earning a groan from him.

"What are you doing?" he asked taken aback by her actions.

"Shh... just imagine that I'm Aaron," she whispered.

That did the trick as he kissed her back harder making her lightheaded. His tongue parted her lips in search for hers as they twirled and danced like they always had.

They heard someone chuckle from behind them and turned to see Aaron leaning against the door.

"Am I interrupting something?" he asked. The door was slightly opened when he came so he didn't bother to knock. He just walked in to see such a beautiful sight.

"Aaron?" Bernard couldn't believe his eyes and rubbed at it to make sure he wasn't dreaming.

"The one and only." He smiled and moved away from the door spreading his arms out for a hug which Bernard obliged.

"I missed you so much." Bernard muttered, his voice almost breaking.

"I know. I missed you just as much," Aaron replied pulling away from Bernard a little bit and then capturing his lips. Their tongue swirled and sucked on each other before Bernard pulled away hazel eyes dark with desire.

"Why are you here? I thought you hated me."

"How could I hate you? I could never hate you. I just needed time to digest what happened. I did my research and learnt more about your kind. That was why I was away for those two weeks because I wanted to understand you."

"So you are not disgusted?"

"No, if anything I love you more than I ever had before."

Bernard's eyes watered. He couldn't believe his ears. Aaron still loved him. He still wanted him. It was a dream come true.

"Have you forgiven me? I mean I kept so many things from you," Bernard gazed at Aaron who shushed him.

"You are not the only one who keeps secrets. I totally understand you. Remember that nobody knows I'm bisexual not even my parents. So how could I not forgive you?"

Ara bit her lip as she watched the two men devour each other's lips. Seeing them dying to feel every inch of each other aroused her to no end but she knew she had to do the right thing.

She needed to leave and give them their privacy no matter how much she was dying to be wrapped in their arms. They didn't want her, they never did.

She made to leave and headed for the door but a hand grabbed her making her stop in her tracks. She turned to see that it was Aaron who was holding her back.

"Why are you leaving?" he asked.

"I don't want to be a third wheel," she replied.

Aaron smiled. "You are not a third wheel, Ara. You are the only woman I've ever fallen in love with."

She gulped. "You love me?"

"Yes I do. I have loved you from the moment I saw you step into my office. Why then should I let you go?"

He then turned to look at Bernard. "You are the only man I will ever love and she's the only woman I will ever love too. Is this ok with you?"

Bernard smiled cupping Aaron's cheek. "I'm perfectly ok with it as long as Ara is."

They both turned to look at Ara whose heart was beating frantically against her chest as she stared at the two loves of her life. This was a dream come true.

"Will you have us both?" Bernard asked.

Bernard was willing to share. There was nothing holding her back anymore.

"Yes," She shouted in joy and stripped out her night robe feeling Aaron's lustful gaze on her causing her clit to throb.

Aaron grabbed her by the waist and kissed her softly, his free hand gripping her ass making her moan against him.

She felt Bernard's presence behind Aaron sucking at his neck.

Aaron's hand reached up to cup her breast, squeezing it. His touch made her feel like she was on fire. She felt him grind his hardened length against her and that was when she knew there was no going back.

She pulled away and grabbed their hands and led them to her bedroom. She sat on the bed her legs spread waiting for them to take action.

She watched as Aaron stripped out of his trousers his eyes focused on her wet cunt.

For so long he had wanted this and here she was spread out in front of him on a platter of gold.

He grabbed each of her thigh and knelt between them. He ran his moist tongue over the edge of her lips teasingly making her gasp.

His tongue then began to thrust in and out of her dripping pussy eating her as if she was his last meal on earth.

She laid on her back, her legs buckling, "Oh god," she let out a loud moan.

She turned her head to the edge of the bed only to see Bernard watching them while stroking himself. She wondered when he had stripped.

Bernard smirked on catching her eyes on his cock and he climbed on the bed. He massaged her breasts, pinching her nipples with his fingers.

Aaron licked her faster and harder giving her no room to catch a breath. She grabbed unto Bernard's rigid cock and wrapped her lips around him causing him to throw his head back and groan in pleasure. She continued to suck on it watching his expression.

Aaron gave her three more hard strokes with his tongue and soon she was cumming. She grabbed unto Bernard's cock as she sucked him off.

Her screams her muffled by Bernard's cock as she felt the muscles of her entire body convulse.

Aaron withdrew from her thighs and stood up, unbuttoning his shirt as he looked down at her.

Bernard removed his cock from her mouth and pulled her by the hands to the bed. She was now fully laying down on the bed, legs spread with cum stained thighs.

She felt Aaron climb unto her, his thick manhood resting between her thighs and he leaned over and kissed her passionately. She wrapped her legs around his back ready for him to enter her.

He entered her gently yet forcefully causing her to scream out in pain and pleasure as he filled her completely.

She brushed her fingers through his hair as he withdrew from her slowly before slamming into her harder.

"Ahh" she groaned digging her nails into his shoulder as he sped up his pace, thrusting into her harder and faster. His thumb rubbed her throbbing clit making her yelp.

"Harder," she whispered gripping the bed spread but he didn't obey, he slowed down his pace and she looked up to see Bernard right behind him resting his hand on Aaron's ass.

The thought of what they were about to do turned her on the more.

Bernard pushed his cock slowly into Aaron's ass making the latter whip his head back.

Aaron continued to fuck her as Bernard entered him. It felt as if Bernard was fucking her too sending shivers down her spine.

Soon the room was filled with sounds of groans and slapping flesh.

The next thing she knew, she was trembling, climaxing and squirting as she spiraled into orgasm, screaming louder than she had ever had.

The two men increased their pace.

Aaron's real undoing was watching Ara orgasm.

He thrust into her hard and fast, exploding his seed into hers as his eyes rolled back into his head.

Bernard continued to fuck him harder and faster until he neared his orgasm. He grabbed unto Aaron's hips and pushed himself deep until he could take it no more and came into Aaron's ass.

Bernard pulled out his cock and collapsed beside a spent Ara. Aaron withdrew from her still sensitive body and collapsed at her other side.

She was now sandwiched in between the two men that she loved.

She kissed the two spent men on the lips feeling happier than ever because there was no place she would rather be than with them.

THE END

Description

Kathy Griffin loves working at the public relations company she has been working for in the past three years. However, when she was promoted to the assistant manager position and she had to work closely with the CEO, Amelia Tuffin, her work didn't seem as fun as before.

Amelia Tuffin is a cold-faced woman and hardly talks about herself. When Kathy realizes that she has a little crush on Amelia, she questions herself.

Axel Astor is a popular actor and signs a contract with Amelia's public relations team. He can't help but be drawn to the fierce but beautiful Amelia and wonders what secret she's carrying?

He finds himself cautious of Kathy when she is close to discovering the secret he harbors but questions himself when he begins to fall for her.

How will they be able to make that decision?

Chapter 1

Kathy Griffin smiled politely at her coworkers as she walked to the cubicle. The room housed ten of them, and although it was large, Kathy wished there were more space between herself and the other employees. Well, at least she could make the tiny cubicle her place. She did spend a lot of time there, working at her desk, and despite the workload, she was always bored. She found that incredible, though, that she had the ability to still search for some form of entertainment even though she barely had enough time on her hands.

Kathy shook the thoughts off and settled in her seat. Her long-time friend, Anna, smiled as soon as she saw her. They both worked at the company, with Anna joining a year after Kathy had. While Kathy wanted to say they had bonded immediately, it wasn't true.

She had judged her wrongly. Anna had walked up to her one day in the bathroom when she was bawling her eyes out for some reason. Ever since then, they had stuck close to each other.

"Hey, you." Anna held out a cup of coffee, and Kathy looked at her appreciatively.

"Hi, what's up?"

Anna shrugged and turned on the desktop. Although she was bubbly and more outgoing, she took her job seriously and always tried to make sure she did all her tasks. "Need to get the brief over with." Then, her face lit up. "Ooh, I heard something."

Kathy sat down and set up her table. She pushed her short hair behind her ears. She had always kept her hair short because it was low maintenance for her that way, but it had been growing, and she didn't have the time for a haircut. "What's that?"

"I heard that Axel Astor is about to be a client with us. That's so crazy!"

Kathy could faintly remember seeing a good-looking man having a press conference about some scandal on television. "Huh, I suppose."

Anna gaped. "Huh?? Really? *THE* Axel Astor is coming to partner with us, which is all you can see. Oh my God, nothing excites you."

Kathy shrugged and opened up a document on her laptop. She had a proposal to print and run by their boss.

Thankfully, Anna decided to stay quiet and focused on her work. The workspace began filling up, and people muttered their hellos. There were days like this. All people wanted to do was sit at their desks and mind their own business. There were also days when they chattered with each other and laughed at funny clients and their weird habits and behaviors.

Kathy gathered the printed papers and put them together in a file. She inhaled a fresh breath of air and stood up from her chair. Her boss unnerved her. It could be because there was always a permanent scowl on Ms. Amelia Tiffin's face. The older woman was probably one of the most beautiful women Kathy had seen, but for some reason, she never smiled.

Kathy wondered why. She owned an entire public relations agency and had such a nice car. Plus, she could nail anybody she wanted, but Kathy hadn't seen her with anyone. At least publicly.

Kathy shook off the thoughts and walked toward the office at the end of the corridor. She politely greeted people as they walked in and out of their offices, but everybody seemed busy. It looked like this Axel of a person was going to be such a demanding person.

Lucy, Amelia's receptionist, raised her eyebrows at her. As fitting, even her receptionist wasn't so friendly either.

Kathy cleared her throat. "Um, hi, I'm here to give Ms. Tiffin the proposal she had asked for."

Lucy barely looked at her. "Drop it here."

Kathy felt her cheeks color. She scrambled to drop the file on the table and then stopped. She had been asked to give Amelia, not Lucy. So why should she drop it? "Actually, I'd rather give Ms. Tiffin it myself."

Lucy stared at her, but Kathy refused to break her resolve. Finally, Lucy raised the phone to her ears and said some things before sending Kathy in.

"Thanks," Kathy said, which was met by a grunt.

She had been in Ms. Amelia's office once, and it still left her in awe of how large it was. What could one person do with all that space? Her entire living room could fit into a corner.

There was a glass wall that overlooked the tall buildings and busy streets of California. Amelia stood in front of it, staring down at the world. Just like she always did.

She turned around when Kathy walked in and barely looked at her. She held out a hand, requesting the document.

Kathy hurriedly gave it to her and stood. Amelia didn't ask her to sit either.

The silence seemed to thicken as Amelia flipped through the proposal, and Kathy felt sweat gather on her forehead. She tried to swallow the lump in their throat and prayed her hands stopped shaking.

Finally, Amelia spoke. "You did this yourself?"

She said it in a tone that gave the sense that she wouldn't appreciate it if Kathy were lying.

"Y-yes. I did."

Amelia nodded and reclined in her chair. She fixed her green eyes on Kathy, and Kathy swallowed, looking everywhere else but her.

"I see. Very well, come work with me."

Kathy felt the lump in her throat grow in size. She laughed nervously. "Well, I do work with you. I'm in the communications department and—"

Amelia cut her short with a wave of her hand. "I mean to work here as my executive assistant. I have been looking for one now, and I believe you can do the job. Judging from the proposal you wrote."

Kathy opened and closed her mouth. She wasn't sure what to say.

Amelia rolled her eyes and stood up. She was a tall woman with such a fit and amazing body that Kathy couldn't stop staring. Her blonde hair was styled in an expensive haircut. "I'll triple your salary, and you travel with me. I don't see how that's better than anything else."

Kathy decided to ignore how arrogant she sounded, and soon enough, she found herself nodding.

Amelia sat back in her chair. "Great. I'll have human resources prepare the contract. You start immediately."

Just like that, Kathy was dismissed. She stumbled out of the office in a daze. She took a quick trip to the bathroom and stared at herself in the mirror. She wished she had worn a better-looking outfit. She was in a white shirt, paired with gray slacks and a patterned vest. It looked so bland compared to the exquisite cream dress Amelia wore.

Kathy walked out of the bathroom and back to her office.

Anna looked at her inquisitively. "You look so dazed. Why?"

Kathy sat down and looked around. She didn't want other people eavesdropping. "I just got promoted."

Anna was confused. "Huh?"

Kathy quickly summarized the ordeal with Amelia and watched as Anna's eyes bulged.

"Oh my gosh, that's awesome. But why are we whispering?" Anna asked in an excited whisper.

"Because I don't want anyone to know about it yet. At least, until it's official."

Anna pouted. "But I'll miss you here."

"I'll miss you too. Don't worry, we'll always catch up outside of work."

Anna hugged her friend and got back to work. Kathy tried to work, but she couldn't concentrate properly. All she could wonder was what it would be like working closely with the *infamous* Ms. Tiffin.

Chapter 2

Kathy looked herself up and down in the mirror one more time. It was her first official day as Amelia's executive assistant, and she wanted to look the part. She had bought a dark purple dress that hugged her slim figure and, at least, made her look more official than she usually did. She had paired the dress with some dark pumps and hoped that she would be able to make the day with them.

Kathy had even tried applying some foundation and mascara, which was good enough. She had never been a huge fan of makeup, simply because she didn't know how to do it.

Her home was a quaint little thing, but it was her comfort zone. It had one bedroom and a living room, and since she was the only one in it, it was good enough for her.

Kathy grabbed her essentials, such as her phone, a new notebook, a pen and the other things she usually carried to work. Amelia hadn't told her what she needed to bring, but human resources had briefed her on her new role's expectations.

Kathy let out a huge breath as she locked the door behind her. She made her way to the large parking lot and spotted her eggplant-colored Volkswagen Beetle. Now that she could afford it, she hoped to change her car soon, but she also wondered if that was a good investment since she would be spending a lot of time traveling with Amelia.

Kathy glanced at the time. She would be early, but she better get on the road already. She drove her car out of the parking lot and made her way onto the busy roads of California.

There was a bit of traffic, and Kathy glanced up to see a large billboard of Axel Astor. It was for some lotion brand, and she couldn't help but wonder why he looked that way. Like a carved statue. Beautiful, but somewhat lifeless.

Since Anna wouldn't stop mentioning him, Kathy finally searched up his name, and there were quite some tasteful articles about him. Turned out she was right, and he did have a scandal. He had managed to beat up some poor guy on some drunken night at the bar.

She wasn't patient enough to see why the altercation had occurred, but she knew it didn't look good for him. Kathy knew that was why he wanted to partner with their agency. To clean up his mess.

She scoffed and drove off as the traffic eased. Just in time, she pulled into the parking lot of the office building at the same time that Amelia did.

She was wearing dark pants with a light blue blouse. Kathy's dismay, she was wearing a white sweater vest which she managed to pull off. Kathy wondered why she had never looked that good in a sweater vest.

Kathy scrambled out of the car and walked up to her. "Good morning, ma'am."

"I expect you to get to the office before me. Don't let it happen again."

"Of course. Never again." Kathy bit her lip as she walked behind her. "This morning, by 8:30 am, you have a meeting with some L'Oréal executives. They want to discuss strengthening their publicity in Africa."

Amelia nodded as she pushed open the door to her office. Lucy stood up to greet her and narrowed her eyes at Kathy. Kathy chose to ignore her and followed Amelia into the office.

"Great. You'll be there for the meeting. Jot down the important points."

Kathy nodded, then realized the woman wasn't looking at her before saying a yes. "By nine o'clock, Axel Astor will be here."

Amelia sat at her desk and frowned. It was just like she was trying to place the name. "Ah, the actor. Of course. I suppose I'll have to see him myself. This is one of our biggest clients, and I can't afford to let some newbie ruin things. Remind me."

"Yes, ma'am." Kathy ran through the rest of the schedule and wondered how Amelia was going to keep up. She wondered for herself also. She was going to be there for most, if not all, the meetings, and it seemed like it was going to be a busy day.

"Until a permanent office is etched out for you, you'll have to make do with the corner over there." Amelia pointed a perfectly manicured finger at a single desk and chair set in the corner.

Kathy walked up to the desk, which was devoid of anything except a laptop and settled right in. She wished she had her personal space, but at least it was far away from Amelia. The woman was starting to unnerve her, and Kathy was afraid of saying the wrong things.

Before she realized, it was already time to meet with the L'Oréal's executives. Working at the ompany for three years, Kathy had had her fair share of meeting with celebrities, but she hadn't really been at such exclusive meetings before. She usually worked on the backend.

Well, polished people with thick, foreign accents soon settled themselves around the table in the conference room, and the meeting began.

Kathy watched in wonder as Amelia took hold of the meeting and commanded the room. She was able to make her client's wishes come through and stood her ground. It was amazing, and Kathy found herself to be in awe. She wrote down the details she felt were most important, and although she wished she were somewhere else, she plastered a smile on her face and nodded her head when it seemed appropriate.

Thankfully, the meeting ended, and they exited the room.

"I need you to go get Axel Astor from his house," Amelia said as she walked down the corridor.

Kathy was taken by surprise. Why should she pick a grown man from his home? Surely, this place wasn't difficult to navigate. Still, she couldn't argue. "Of course, ma'am."

"My driver will take you. The address has been sent to him. But he must come back to me immediately so that you'll get a ride with Axel. You have to leave now." Amelia walked into her office, leaving Kathy standing outside.

She blinked and began the walk to the lobby. Thankfully, Amelia's driver was sitting in a chair and stood up as soon as he spotted her.

They got into the car, and Kathy resisted the urge to sink into the soft seat. They made their way to the posh area of the city. Kathy couldn't help but notice how similar all the houses were. It would be very easy to go astray in that kind of place.

The driver dropped her in front of a huge mansion and drove off. Kathy huffed and hopped to God that the man was at least home.

She walked up to the door and pushed the doorbell. Soon enough, she heard some footsteps defending the stairs, and a slim brunette wrapped in a sheer robe opened the door. She raised a perfectly arched eyebrow at Kathy.

Kathy found herself stuttering at the woman's boobs seemed to stare at her in the face. Finally, she gained her composure. "Hi, I'm from Tiffin's agency, and I'm here for Mr. Astor."

The brunette smiled, seemingly unharmed. "Oh, I'm Tiffany. Come in." I'll go tell him." The woman sashayed up the stairs, and Kathy was left alone.

She opened her mouth as she took in her surroundings. Everything screamed expensive. There was a large painting hanging above the fireplace, and Kathy wondered if that was such a wise decision.

The furniture looked like it could pass as a marshmallow, and there was a shining oak coffee table right in the middle. Medals and plagues lined a shelf right beside the door, and Kathy knew that there was a reason it was the first thing one saw as soon as they entered the house.

"Damn. This is crazy, Kathy muttered to herself as she stared at the bear head rug. She hoped it was at least faux fur.

Kathy heard footsteps coming down the stairs and turned to see whether it was Tiffany bearing news. However, it was Axel Astor, coming down the stairs in all his glory.

Kathy felt the air leave her body. She had seen pictures of Axel, but mostly at face level. None of them could do justice to what she was seeing now.

He had a towel wrapped around his waist as water dripped down his body. He shook his head, and water droplets flew from his dark hair. Kathy stared at his lips as the moisture made them look even plumper.

She swallowed and tried not to look at the towel, dangerously getting lower.

Axel held out his hand. "Hi, I'm Axel. I'm sorry, I'm getting ready. You can make yourself comfy, and I'll be done in a jiffy."

Kathy could only swallow and nod. Tiffany climbed down the stairs and put an arm around Axel's neck.

He looked genuinely surprised to see her. "Brittany? What are you doing here."

Kathy looked somewhere else as Tiffany's jaw slacked open. "It's Tiffany, you ass." She ran up the stairs and gathered her clothes. As soon as she came down, she smacked Axel soundly on his cheeks and walked out of the house in a huff.

The silence between Kathy and Axel stretched, and Kathy wondered who was more stunned. She or him. "Um, I'll just wait here." She quickly sat on the couch and looked away from him. Her cheeks burned with embarrassment for him. "

"Yeah. I'll be back." Axel walked up the stairs slowly, as if he couldn't believe what had happened to him.

Kathy bit her lip and glanced to make sure he was gone before she snickered to herself. It's not every day you see a famous actor getting smacked right in the face. She couldn't wait to tell Anna what had happened.

Thankfully, Axel was back in some jeans and a t-shirt in record time. "Come on, let's go," he said to Kathy, beckoning for her to follow him.

They made their way to his garage, and Kathy felt her mouth open as the automatic door did open, revealing the wide array of sports cars.

Axel grinned at her reaction and pointed the key at a dark red Ferrari. "I'll be taking that today."

He drove the car out, and Kathy opened the door to get in. With that, they sped away.

Chapter 3

The journey back to the office was quicker than she had expected, and Kathy was thankful for it. Axel was a wild driver, and she felt her nails digging into her seat each time she heard the car roar louder. Still, she didn't complain and let out a breath of relief when she saw their company insight.

"This way," Kathy said as she led him up the stairs to Amelia's office. He had worn a baseball hat and some glasses in an attempt to disguise. Luckily for him, everyone at the office seemed too busy to take a closer look at him.

Kathy knocked on Amelia's office door and stepped in when she heard the woman ask her to go on.

Amelia stood up with a smile. "Axel. It's lovely to see you."

Axel stepped into the room and kissed her on the cheek. "I must say the same. You look quite different from what I had expected. In a good way."

Amelia smiled politely. It wasn't the first time she had heard such a compliment.

Kathy stared at the two of them. Although it seemed like this was their first-time meeting, she could have sworn that a flash of familiarity went between them. She shook it off and proceeded to leave the room.

"Oh no. Stay." Amelia pointed at Kathy.

They all settled on a couch as Lucy poured steaming coffee for them. Kathy inhaled the rich smell and sipped the piping hot beverage.

"So, I have run through your file, and your agent has spoken to me about the entire issue, but I wanted to hear from you. So tell me. What would you like us to do for you?"

"I mean, I just want the whole issue to die down. And I want to be the most polished version of myself."

Amelia nodded. "You do realize that you also have a huge role to play. You need to be on your best behavior."

Axel straightened and nodded. "I understand. I will be."

They spoke for some time, and Kathy tried to write all she could write down, but she got distracted staring at Axel. His face was something to behold. It was smooth, yet the jarring lines of his jaw gave him a rugged look.

He had well-toned arms, and she wondered how much he had to work for them. Kathy had noticed a thick scar on his neck and wondered where he had gotten such a puckering scar. It seemed like the only flaw in his otherwise perfect exterior.

Thankfully, the meeting ended, and Axel stood up. "You'll be seeing a lot of me."

Kathy didn't know if he directed the comment to her or Amelia, but he was looking at her, so she nodded. "Of course. I look forward to that."

Amelia walked him out, and Kathy remained in the office. Her stomach rumbled, and she became aware she hadn't eaten anything all morning. She bit her lips and held her stomach. She had developed an ulcer earlier and could feel the pain in her belly increase.

When Amelia walked back into the office, Kathy tried to hide the discomfort on her face, but her boss had already narrowed her eyes at her. "What's the problem?"

"Oh, nothing." Kathy's voice sounded strangled. She could have been able to get away with it, but her belly decided to let out a loud growl.

Amelia lifted a brow and grabbed her purse. "Why don't we grab lunch together? We can go to my spot. We can't have you fall over and collapse now, can we?"

Kathy opened her mouth to argue. She decided that it wouldn't be wise. She nodded and followed Amelia as they walked out of the office.

They didn't have to drive too far at all. As soon enough, the car was parked right in front of a five-star restaurant.

Kathy had expected to go to the local sandwich shop, not this high end-looking place.

The host smiled at Amelia and greeted her with reverence. He led them to a private booth and settled down.

"I'll have the lamb chops and rice, please," Amelia said to the waiter.

"I'll have the same too," Kathy said when the waiter turned to take her order.

There would have been an awkward silence if not for the soft music playing in the background, at least from Kathy's side.

It was weird for her, sitting at some nice restaurant with her boss whom she hadn't said more than five words before the present week.

She was grateful when they brought their meal. At least, that was something for her to focus on.

"You shouldn't skip breakfast," Amelia said with a frown.

"I just wanted to make it in time."

"It's no good if you have an issue at work." Amelia looked at her for a while before settling with her food.

They ate quietly, with Kathy scanning the restaurant with her eyes as they ate. It was nice, for a change, to be somewhere like that.

"We have a fundraising event to attend this weekend. You will be accompanying me."

It was not a question, and Kathy could only not in response to Amelia's statement. "Of course. That's no problem."

***

Anna scrunched up her nose and shook her head. "Yeah, this won't work. You need a better outfit."

Kathy was panicking, and she groaned. "Oh gosh, this is my last formal dress. I don't have anything else."

Anna put a hand on her hips. "How come you're telling me now? We could have gotten something during the week. Now the day is here."

"I thought I had something to wear. I was so sure I had something to wear."

"Well, now you don't."

Kathy sank to her bed miserably. She wished she could cancel but she knew Amelia would have her head. She couldn't dare.

There was a thud at the door, and Anna raised her brows. "Are you expecting someone?" she asked.

Kathy shook her head and stood up. She walked toward the door and looked into the peephole. There was a man in a uniform, holding something that looked like a box.

She opened the door carefully. "May I help you?"

"Delivery for a Miss Kathy Griffin?"

"That's me."

"Okay. Please sign here. And here."

Kathy signed and collected the box. She shut the door behind her and walked toward a very curious Anna.

"Ooh, what is that?"

Inquisitively, Kathy gently opened the box and gasped when she saw the content.

"Oh my gosh," Anna's eyes widened.

Kathy brought out a light pink dress that sparkled faintly under the light. There was an open back, and the neckline plunged a little.

Also in the box were some black heels and a black suede purse.

"Scandalous. I love it." Anna nodded as she held up the dress.

Kathy noticed that there was a small note in the box. *I assume you don't have a dress.*

Yep. Definitely sounded like her.

Chapter 4

Kathy was supposed to drive to meet Amelia at her home, and if she was honest, she was a little curious to see where her boss lived.

Amelia's home was all alone in its surroundings. Kathy shivered as she drove up to the large house. She wondered how the woman lived all by herself in such a large house in the middle of nowhere.

Kathy got out of her car and rang the bell.

"Coming," A cheerful voice rang out, and an older woman opened the door.

She wore cleaning attire and was holding a vacuum cleaner in her hand. "Ah, you must be Kathy. Come in, come in. Ms. Tiffin said you should wait for her in the living room."

Kathy nodded and stepped into the room. She wobbled a bit in her heels but soon gained balance. Her cheeks reddened when she saw that the cleaner had seen her falter.

She sat gingerly on a dark red leather couch and folded her arms, waiting. She had expected the house to be devoid of character and completely bare, but Kathy was surprised to see the hints of personality around the house.

There were photo frames from the various stages of Amelia's life, and Kathy smiled when she saw a very chubby prepubescent Amelia. She couldn't imagine the woman to be less perfect than ever.

There was a snow globe on the mantle, and Kathy stood up and walked toward it.

Right in the middle of the globe was a caricature of Amelia in a snowy town. Kathy shook it and giggled as the caricature tumbled alongside Emilia.

"A friend in London gave it to me." Kathy was startled by the sudden voice and quickly dropped the globe before turning around. "I'm sorry." She started, but her voice faded away.

Amelia wore a black dress that flowed out around her waist. There was a single strap, and it showed off her toned skin. Her hair had been curled around her face, and there was bright red lipstick on her lips.

Kathy's heart thumped, and she was afraid that Amelia would hear her. She was fierce and beautiful all at the same time.

Amelia nodded her head approvingly. "The dress suits you. Hold on."

She walked to Kathy and turned Kathy around as she adjusted the cloth. Kathy closed her eyes and inhaled her perfume. It smelled like blackberries and seduction.

What was wrong with her? She couldn't possibly be attracted to her boss.

Her skin sizzled when Amelia had touched her, even after the woman stepped away.

"We need to leave," Amelia said and walked away from her.

Kathy followed her behind as they got into the car.

Nicholas, who was Amelia's driver, as Kathy had learned, greeted them and soon, they were on their way.

Kathy fixed her gaze on the view outside the car, and she tried not to acknowledge the presence of Amelia. On the other hand, her budding feelings.

She couldn't believe that was happening to her. She didn't want to feel that way for her boss. Not when she was so closed off and cold to the people around her.

Thankfully, Amelia didn't say much other than to prep her on the type of people they would converse with at the party. Clients.

They got to the venue, and Kathy was in awe of how large it was. Lights were on every corner, and even the parking lot was lit up.

Various scents of perfumes filled the parking lot as people got out from their luxurious cars in luxurious dresses.

Kathy followed Amelia, and she blushed as men stared at her, impressed. Even though she was attracted to both men and women, she didn't get much attention from either, which was all new to her.

They put some identifying wristbands around their hands and went into the venue.

Violin music played as they entered the event center, and tables were arranged in each corner of the hall with numbers on them.

Kathy glanced at her wristband. They were placed at number seven.

"Oh, great," Amelia muttered under her breath as she spotted the table.

Kathy followed her gaze and looked at the two women already at the table. They seemed to have spotted Amelia and were muttering behind their hands. She wondered who they were.

With a confident stride, Amelia walked up to the table.

One of the two women, dressed in a hot pink gown, smiled at Amelia. "Oh, what a surprise to see you here. We thought you would never attend public events again."

Kathy tried to keep her face neutral, but she wondered what the woman was on about.

"Lisa," Amelia said in a tone that could pass as a warning or a greeting. "Joleen. It's nice to see you again."

Joleen smiled, but her face barely changed. Kathy suspected it was because of too much Botox, maybe. "Of course, darling. You look the same."

Kathy picked up on the hostility and sat gingerly in her seat. She wasn't sure what was going on but knew it would be best if she just stayed quiet.

Thankfully, the hall began filling up, and the woman got distracted as they made their comments on people's outfits.

"Hello, ladies." Kathy turned around at the sound of the voice. It was Axel, and he was wearing a gold-colored tux tailored specifically for him.

"Mr. Astor. It's quite astonishing to see you here." Amelia genuinely looked surprised. Kathy remembered that she had told him to stay out of public events in the meantime. Clearly, he didn't heed her words.

"Ah well, I can't help but be drawn to the public scene. Anyway, I'll see you two around. Kathy, you look lovely," Axel said before walking away.

Kathy felt her heart skip a beat as she watched his receding figure.

The hall filled up, and the event began. The host, an elderly woman who seemed quite delighted to be there, said something, but Kathy wasn't really listening. She was stunned by the number of famous people in the room. It was all new to her.

"So, is this your new eye candy? You haven't had any of those since you came out." Lisa threw a jab at Amelia. The table had been silent until the two women spoke, and Kathy was taken aback. She hadn't known about her boss's sexuality, but suddenly it made sense to her.

Amelia's face was blank, and she said in a quiet voice. "Please, excuse me." She stood up and left the room.

Kathy watched her receding figure and turned to face the two women. "I don't know who Ms. Amelia is to you, but she's a hard-working woman and is twice the person you are. Her sexuality doesn't concern you. You should be worried about your husbands, or lack of." With a huff, Kathy left the table.

Her heart was racing, and she couldn't believe she had said what she had said. There was no way that had come out of her mouth, but it had.

She strolled out of the building and rubbed her arms as the chilly cold hit her. It was midnight and much colder outside than it was inside.

Kathy looked around, but Amelia was nowhere to be found. She brought her phone to dial the number. It rang, but nobody picked.

Kathy turned to the back of the building and was nervous to see that the place was devoid of people.

"Amelia? Um, Miss Tiffin?" Kathy called out into the dark.

The bushes rustled, and she felt her heartbeat race faster. She took a step backward as the rustle became louder. A large black dog appeared from the bushes.

Kathy gasped at the size of the dog. It didn't look like a regular dog. Its fangs were much longer and looked more dangerous. Also, its fur was longer than a domestic dog. Kathy tried to convince herself otherwise, but something told her that she was looking at a real-life wolf.

It was bleeding from its side, and that was when Kathy ran away from the place.

Panting heavily, she ran up the stairs by the sides and pushed open a heavy door leading to the rooftop.

Standing all by herself was Amelia. She turned to look at who it was and seemed surprised to see Kathy.

"How did you find me?"

Kathy shook her head, struggling to catch her breath. "Honestly, I don't know."

Amelia frowned. "Are you all right?"

"Yes." Kathy straightened. "Just trying to catch my breath."

Amelia nodded and turned to stare at the view of the city. Everything was so high up from here, and Kathy didn't get as close to the balcony as Amelia was. She was a little scared of heights.

"You know, I came out only a few years ago. I was so scared it would be in the tabloids. Thankfully, nobody seemed to care much. Well, nobody except California's exclusives." Amelia spat the words out, irritated. "Quite embarrassing for them, hypocritical too. They are accepting of everyone except me. I haven't dated anyone since I divorced my ex-husband years ago."

Kathy was surprised by this news. She hadn't known Amelia had been married. Still, she kept quiet. She didn't want the woman to stop.

Amelia let out a laugh devoid of humor. "It doesn't matter how lonely it gets. I'd rather be all by myself than to be mocked."

Kathy felt her heartache for her. "It doesn't matter what they say. I think you are such a spectacular woman. If no one wants to be with you, it's simply because they aren't good enough."

Amelia laughed. "Oh, please. I'm not going to fire you if you;re honest."

Kathy took a step closer and looked at her. For the first time, she could see cracks in the armor that Amelia Tiffin had created. "I mean, you can be quite a meanie sometimes, and you aren't exactly the nicest person, but I think if you allow yourself, you could be the kindest person ever."

Amelia looked into her eyes as unshed tears glimmered in them. Kathy felt drawn to the older woman. It was like a spell that couldn't be broken.

"And I think you are the most attractive woman ever," Kathy whispered as she lifted a hand to wipe the tears in Amelia's eyes.

Slowly, Amelia closed her eyes and leaned in. She moved closer until her lips touched Kathy's. And sparks flew in the air as they kissed under the midnight sky.

Chapter 5

Kathy stalled outside the office building on shaky legs. She wasn't sure how she could face Amelia after what had happened between them, but she knew she had to.

She inhaled a deep breath and made her way into the building. Kathy greeted some workers on the way and was shocked when they responded to her. Usually, she was met with a grunt or a halfhearted hello.

Lucy still hadn't warmed up to her, but at least she wasn't given her death glares anymore.

Kathy knocked on the door and entered when Amelia told her to come in.

"Good morning," Kathy said, although she was surprised to see Axel sitting across from Amelia.

Amelia looked normal, and she put on a small smile. "Morning. Please sit." Then she addressed them both. "I must say, while I thought the public appearance was too soon, it did a little good for you, Axel. Let's keep it that way, fresh and clean."

Axel nodded, then winced.

Kathy looked at him with concern. "Are you okay?"

Axel nodded and gave a stiff smile. "Yeah. Just hurt my side a little, that's all. It's nothing."

Something pricked at the back of Kathy's mind, and she frowned, trying to place it. But she decided to let it go. "All right. Take it easy."

Amelia nodded in agreement. "Yeah, go to the hospital if it hurts."

Axel shook his head firmly. "Nah, it's just a small scratch."

"Well then," Amelia said. "Kathy, Axel has a promotional shoot today. Please accompany him. I want to ensure I don't miss out on all the details."

"All right, of course."

Axel stood up. "Well, I have to run some quick errands. Kathy, I'll be back here real soon."

Kathy nodded and smiled as he left the room. When the door was shut behind him, the room was smaller.

Kathy swallowed and looked everywhere else but at Amelia.

Amelia stood up and cleared her throat. "What happened on Saturday..."

Kathy bit her lip. "I am so sorry, ma'am. I promise it won't happen again."

Amelia raised a brow. "Really? You didn't like it?"

Kathy's face turned red." What? No, I did, but I just assumed... you didn't."

Amelia moved closer to Kathy and leaned on the table, right in front of her seat. Kathy could smell her perfume and see the star birthmark on her neck. She wanted to kiss it.

"Well, I did like it. Very much. Can I do it again?"

Kathy swallowed and nodded. She leaned in closer and allowed Amelia to take her lips in hers.

A moan escaped Kathy's lips as Amelia kissed her with an urgent fervency. They stood up at once and made their way to the couch.

Amelia leaned over Kathy and trailed kisses down her neck. Kathy felt like someone had set fire to her blood, and it was boiling. She couldn't get enough of it.

Amelia gently slipped a hand into Kathy's dress and traced lines over her thighs.

Feeling confident, Kathy moved Amelia's hands upward, looking into her eyes. Kathy put a hand inside Amelia's blouse and stroked her firm breasts.

Amelia began working her hands on Kathy's clit, looking into her eyes as Kathy grew breathless.

Kathy's gasp became fainter as Amelia worked her fingers faster and quietly; she orgasmed onto Amelia's hands.

Amelia chuckled and brought some tissue paper to clean up. "Well, how was that?"

Kathy swallowed and nodded. "Good. Really good."

Then Amelia kissed her on the cheek. "Anytime."

A loud bang came at the door, followed by Axel's voice. The two women scrambled to look normal, and Amelia told Axel to enter.

Axel lifted a brow at the tow of them standing stiffly. "Are you okay?"

"Yes, yes. You need to get going." Amelia said and went back to her desk.

Kathy nodded and followed Axel out the door, avoiding his curious gaze.

He had brought another car, but at least it was a normal-looking jeep. Kathy guessed he didn't really want to draw any attention to himself.

They got into the car and made their way onto the busy roads of California.

"So, do you want to say why your cheeks are so flushed?"

Kathy opened and closed her mouth before placing a hand on her cheek. "No, they're not. I'm fine, really,"

Axel shrugged. "All right then. Well, you are about to see me in my element, so you may be more flushed than this. Prepare yourself."

Kathy rolled her eyes at his smirk. "I'll be fine." She was a little curious to see what Axel was like in front of the camera.

They pulled up at some open set. There were cameras everywhere, and people were pacing all over the place.

Axel walked toward a woman, and Kathy followed him. She ignored the glances people gave her and tried to remain as professional as possible.

"Damien, this is Kathy. Kathy, this is Damien, the director."

Damien was a bald man with impeccable fashion taste and a bright smile to go with it. "Oh, lovely. My pleasure." Then he turned to Axel. "The shoot is about to begin. You need to get ready. Go to the dressing room. There are people there already."

Axel turned to Kathy and winked at her. "Want to come? It'll be fun."

Kathy ignored his suggestive tone and rolled her eyes. "No thanks."

Axel spoke. "Actually, I think it'll be nice for you to go with me. I heard you are supposed to take notes or something."

Kathy couldn't help but agree with him. "All right, Let's go."

They made their way to a trailer, and when Axel opened the door, Kathy could have easily mistaken the interior for a small house.

People rushed at Damien to take him to get ready. Kathy slowly followed them behind, taking in the room.

She wondered if this was a one-time something and if so, they had done a good job putting it together.

Axel sat in front of a mirror while a woman touched his face with some powder.

"So, you do this a lot?"

Axel looked at her in the mirror. "What? The shoots? Yeah. Before I became an actor, I was a model."

Kathy nodded. It did make sense. He seemed to fit perfectly in the whole scene.

Kathy decided to go all out and asked, "So, why did you beat up a man?"

Axel pursed his lips and looked around. "I'll like to be alone for a few minutes. I'll be down soon." They had dressed him in simple outfits, but it only seemed to make him look even better.

Soon enough, the trailer was empty except for them. Axel turned around to look at her. "The truth?"

Kathy nodded.

"Well, I beat him up because he kept calling this woman a whore, since she wouldn't give him her number. It was all ridiculous to me."

"Why didn't you ever say that was why?"

Axel laughed. "When you are a public figure like me, nothing is ever good enough. It didn't matter the story I told. The tabloids already decided the story to publish."

Kathy stared at him for a moment. She felt bad that he had to be in that type of position, not to be able to defend his name.

Axel winced and held his side. Kathy frowned and walked up to him. "What's the problem?"

Axel shook his head. "It's nothing really."

Kathy narrowed her eyes and pulled his hands off his side. She slowly lifted his shirt and stared in horror at what was right before her. There was a blood-soaked bandage wrapped around him, and Kathy unwrapped it to reveal a deep wound.

"What the hell?" she swore.

Axel tried to hide it from her. "It's nothing. I just fell."

Kathy scoffed. "Fell my ass. That doesn't look like a wound you get from falling."

Axel looked away. "Just leave it."

Kathy had the sense that he didn't want to talk about it. So she decided to let the issue go. "But I'm going to have to redress that. Or you go to the hospital."

Axel shook his head. "No, I'm not going to the hospital. You can redress it, thanks."

Kathy crossed her fingers and hoped that there was a first aid box somewhere around. Thankfully, she found a box in a cabinet and took some gauze, a fresh set of bandages and some balm to ease the sting.

She cleaned the wound as gently as she could because she knew it had to hurt a lot. When it looked like it wouldn't develop any infection, she wrapped it in the bandage.

"All done. After this, you need to go home and rest as much as you can. Really."

Axel grinned. "Geez, you sound like my mom. Yeah yeah, I will. Thanks again."

A knock on the trailer door signified that it was time for the shoot to begin.

Axel exited the room, and Kathy trailed behind him.

She sat in a corner as they offered her some iced tea while she watched Axel pose for the camera. He was a natural and worked perfectly well with the director, so much that they were in sync.

Kathy sipped her tea and blushed as she remembered her moment with Amelia. She wasn't sure what was going on between them. She wished they could come out and say what it really was, but Kathy was too scared to make the first move. It hurt her that there was the possibility it could be something very casual for Amelia. She didn't want to think much about it and brought out her notebook to write all there was to write.

Thankfully, the shoot didn't take too long, and Axel shook hands with the director before going to meet Kathy.

"Hey, you."

"Hey."

"Want to grab lunch?"

Kathy was taken aback by how offhandedly Axel said it, but she nodded in response. She was quite hungry and made a mental note to stop skipping breakfast.

They hopped into Axel's car, and he drove them to some takeout restaurant, where they ordered cheeseburgers.

Kathy admitted that she was a little surprised he could order something as normal as that. "So where are we going?"

Axel smirked. "I want to take you to my spot."

Kathy laughed. "You have a spot? Well, let's see where it is."

They drove for a little while and finally rounded into an open field.

There was a wooden cart in the corner, and it had a covering that shielded them from the sun. There were packed sacks in the cart to soften the seat, and the two made themselves comfortable.

It was quite nice for Kathy to rest in a field of daffodils.

"It's so peaceful here."

Axel nodded as he closed his eyes. "Yeah, it is. I come here sometimes to get away from the buzz of it all."

Kathy nodded. "Yeah, I understand."

They fell into a comfortable silence before Axel finally spoke again. "So, tell me. How can I get Amelia to fall in love with me?"

Kathy barked out a surprised laugh. "Are you serious?"

Axel laughed also. "Well, half-serious. Maybe not love, but damn she is one fine woman."

Kathy smiled and nodded. "She is." Surprisingly, she didn't feel as jealous as she thought. She assumed it had to do with the fact that Amelia wasn't attracted to men.

Kathy turned to look at Axel and was surprised to see him watching her. "What?"

Axel smiled softly. "Nothing. You're quite an attractive woman yourself."

Kathy huffed. "Ha-ha, not really."

"No, really. You have these gorgeous large eyes that make you look so innocent."

Kathy looked at him. "Thank you."

Axel moved closer to her. Close enough that she could see the tiny bump on his nose, and she didn't fight it when he finally kissed her.

The kiss was long, slow and sweet. But Kathy knew that it was different from what she had felt with Amelia. Kissing Amelia was like loading herself with an explosion.

Finally, they separated, and Axel smiled. "I want to invite you and Amelia for dinner tonight."

Kathy lifted a brow. "You'll have to do that yourself."

All right. Let's go." Axel held out a hand to Kathy, and they made their way back to the car.

The drive back to the office wasn't awkward at all. If anything, Kathy felt like Axel was an old friend. They sang to the popular songs on the radio as they drove.

They pulled up to the office, chattering like old friends. They ran into Anna on the way, who was gaping like a fish when she saw Axel.

Kathy decided to take the chance. "Oh Axel, this is my best friend, Anna. Anna, this is—"

"Axel Astor. Heck, I know. It's nice to meet you. So nice." Kathy held out a hand to shake him.

Instead, Axel took the hand to his lips and kissed it gently. Kathy snickered quietly when she saw Anna's eyes bulged. Well, at least her friend had a story to tell everyone. They waved goodbye and continued on their way to the office.

Amelia wasn't surprised to see them, but she smiled when they came into her office. "You're back. How was it?"

"He is a natural." Kathy smiled and dropped the note in front of Amelia.

"You flatter me. Anyway, I was hoping I could invite you to dinner this evening. I'll cook. It's just a way of me showing my appreciation."

Amelia frowned. "Oh, Mr. Astor, if anything, we should be the ones thanking you."

Axel shook his head. "Of course not. I insist. And please, call me Axel."

Amelia pondered for a bit, and slowly, she nodded. "All right. What time?"

"Seven o'clock. I'll be sending the address to you."

They said their goodbyes, and Axel excused himself, saying he had a yoga appointment.

When they were left alone, Amelia stood up and grinned mischievously. "So, where were we?"

And after that, she pleased Kathy all over again.

Chapter 6

Kathy held onto Amelia's hands as Nicholas drove them to Axel's home. Amelia smiled back at her and squeezed her hand.

Kathy was a little disappointed when she released her hand as soon as they pulled up in front of Axel's house. But she didn't let that trouble her too much.

They walked toward the front door, and Axel opened the door after they rang the bell.

"Hey! You're here." He was wearing a shirt, and some slacks with the first two buttons of the shirt popped open.

Kathy had worn a dress with ruffled and was glad when Amelia said it was pretty. The older woman had worn a jumpsuit with pumps. Casual, but quite fitting for her.

"We brought wine." Amelia held up a bottle of expensive wine.

Axel grinned and collected the bottle. "Come right in."

They made their way to the dining table, where it had been set already, and there were candles lit around.

They were alone in the house, and Axel put on some soft music in the background.

They laughed as he served them the meal he had cooked. Kathy was surprised that the food was quite good and even decided to go for a second round.

She was glad to see that Amelia was smiling and seemed quite loosened up that night. It was something she didn't get to see quite often, and she thanked Axel mentally for the opportunity.

"Come on, drink some more." Kathy laughed as she topped Amelia's cup with more wine. She admitted she was a little tipsy, but Kathy was also glad for the alcohol in her system. It made her a little bold.

Many more glasses in, the three of them were giggling and staggering as the alcohol kicked into their system.

They made their way to the living room and tried to focus on the program showing.

Amelia looked at Kathy with want and began kissing her, ignoring Axel's presence.

Axel whistled. "Wow. Who knew you guys were together? This is hot."

Kathy giggled as Amelia kissed her.

Axel shook his head. "Man, can I join you guys?"

Amelia turned her head to him. "Do you want to?"

"Hell yeah."

Amelia turned to look at Kathy to see if it was okay with her. Kathy nodded as she stared at Axel with lust. She admitted she didn't like him as she did for Amelia, but she was attracted to him.

"Fuck yes." Axel stood up from his seat and made his way to them. He trailed kisses down Kathy's neck, and Amelia kissed her lips.

Kathy moaned at the sensation and knew that was an invitation for them.

Amelia reached into Kathy's dress, and Kathy massaged her breasts. Axel wasn't too behind either, and he gently grabbed Kathy's breasts and gave them a little squeeze.

"Let's go upstairs," Kathy whispered with want. They all followed Axel to his bedroom and were comforted that the bedroom was big enough for all of them.

Amelia pushed Kathy onto the bed and worked her mouth on Kathy's vagina. Kathy gasped as she kissed Axel and arched her back for him to grab her breasts.

"Can I?" Axel looked at the two women for permission. Both Kathy and Amelia nodded, and he grabbed a condom.

He wore it over his member and gently teased Kathy at her entrance. Amelia wasn't left behind as Kathy stroked her clit, looking into her eyes.

Slowly, Axel began moving into Kathy, falling into a rhythmic pulse. Kathy focused on pleasuring Amelia as the three of them were joined together by passion.

As they moved faster and moans escaped their lips, they rode on the wings of ecstasy as they came together.

***Kathy slowly opened her eyes and winced as the headache hit her. Memories of last night rushed through her head, and she blushed, remembering what had occurred between them. She liked it, though, and was glad she could bond more with Amelia.

Kathy glanced at the clock by the bed. It was a few minutes after two in the morning. Her throat felt like a desert, and she needed a cold glass of water.

She grabbed a robe and wrapped it around her body. Kathy looked around and realized that neither Axel nor Amelia were in the room.

She gently made her way down the stairs, just in case they were asleep somewhere else. Kathy heard some noise from the living room and stopped in her steps. Wondering what was happening.

She rounded the curve leading to the living room and gasped when she took in what was before her. The living room was completely upturned, and the furniture had been torn to pieces.

Kathy was frozen with fear when she saw something that threatened her sanity. Right in front of her were four large wolves, fighting with each other.

With a gasp, Kathy hit the floor with a loud noise, and everything went black.

***For the second time that day, Kathy's eyes fluttered open. She saw a very scared Amelia looking at her and a concerned Axel holding a glass of water for her.

Kathy groaned as she sat uprightly.

"No, no, just lie down." Amelia kissed her forehead and lowered her down onto the bed.

Memories of what she had seen rushed to Kathy, and she whimpered in fear. "I saw... I saw."

Axel held her hand. "Kathy, it's okay. We know."

Kathy frowned. "You know what?"

"That you saw wolves. Werewolves." Amelia bit her lip in guilt and stared at Kathy.

Kathy felt a sickening realization in her stomach. She curled into a ball and backed away from them. Her heart broke when Amelia's eyes welled up with tears, but her fear overshadowed everything. "Oh my gosh. This isn't real. Werewolves aren't real."

Axel was firm. "Kathy, listen. Could you allow us to explain? At least for your sanity."

Kathy opened her mouth to speak, but she decided to stay quiet.

Axel took the cue and spoke. "I'm a werewolf. There's no other way to say this, and so is Amelia. Before you say anything, we didn't know either of us were werewolves before we officially met. So this isn't some plan or game. Those other werewolves you saw were trying to attack us. I guess they smelled us out. We dealt with them, but not at a cost. The living room is in disarray, and my wound reopened. But it's nothing I can't fix."

Amelia held Kathy's quivering hands. "Kathy, I didn't mean to bring you into this. I didn't mean to fall for you. I wanted to keep that part of my life away from you because I was scared that you wouldn't be able to handle it. I'm scared that

I'm right about that. I perfectly understand if you hate me and want me gone."

Kathy's teeth shook as she closed her eyes. Her lover was a werewolf. Or was it vixen? She didn't know. Kathy swallowed, and she looked into Amelia's eyes. She seemed genuine, and Kathy knew that the next words she spoke would determine everything else.

"Okay."

Amelia's face contorted with confusion. "Okay?"

"Okay. You are werewolves. Anything else I need to know?"

Axel smiled and shook his head. "Well, I have a double-jointed elbow, but that's all."

Kathy shook her head and looked at Amelia. "I'm going to be honest with you. This is still freaky for me, and it'll take some time for me to warm up to the idea, but I don't really care as long as it's still you, Amelia. I don't want anyone else, and your werewolf identify won't change that."

Tears dropped from Amelia's eyes as she hugged Kate tightly. "Oh, it's always been you."

Kathy turned to look at Axel. "So you were the wolf I saw? At the fundraising event?"

Axel nodded. Yep. "It was me. They attacked me at the event too."

Kathy nodded and turned to look at Amelia. She looked even more beautiful when she cried.

Axel quietly exited the room, leaving the two women alone.

Amelia gathered Kathy in her arms and hugged her to herself. "You know, I'm thirty-five. Is that too old for you?"

Kathy laughed. "You are only five years older than I am. Plus, I don't really care."

Amelia turned to look at her with a serious look on her face. "Will you be my woman? I've never uttered those words out loud, but I don't think I want to say that to anyone else but you."

Kathy bit her lip and slowly kissed Amelia on her lips. "Yes. Over and over again. I want to be."

"Good. So I can do this?" Amelia smiled mischievously as she lowered herself to Kathy's thighs. She slowly pulled apart the robe, revealing a very naked Kathy.

Kathy blushed with embarrassment but was soon gasping with pleasure as Amelia worked her tongue into her. She could get used to that.

Amelia gently played with her already hard nipples as Kathy came with a loud gasp.

"Well, I should return the favor," Kathy said as she gently pushed Amelia down.

She laughed at the surprised look on Amelia's face and pulled off her clothes. She sat on the older woman, making sure that their vagina lips were locked as she began to move on her.

Amelia moaned, and Kathy took that cue to quicken her pace. She knew that their moans were all over the place, but Kathy didn't care. All she wanted was that moment with Amelia, and as their bodies shook together, she knew she had it.

Interlocked, they lay on the bed, wrapped in each other's arms. Amelia turned to look at her. "I can't wait to show you to everyone. I want to be loud about you. None of that hiding thing."

Kathy smiled and kissed her lips. "I can't wait to show you off too. To tell everyone that you are mine."

And truly, she was.

THE END